Also by Clifford B. Bowyer

Continuing the Passion
Beyond Belief
Snapped
Gen-Ops

The Warlord Trilogy
Falestia
Falestian Heir

Fall of the Imperium Trilogy
The Impending Storm
The Changing Tides
The Siege of Zoldex

The Adventures of Kyria
The Child of Prophecy
The Awakening
The Mage's Council
The Shard of Time
Trapped in Time
Quest for the Shard
The Spread of Darkness
The Apprentice of Zoldex
The Darkness Within
The Rescue of Nezbith
The Responsibility of Arifos
Full Circle

Ilfanti and the Orb of Prophecy
Tales of the Council of Elders
(Ilfanti's Tale, Ariness's Tale, Bonus Tale)

SNAPPED

by

Clifford B. Bowyer

HOLLISTON, MASSACHUSETTS

SNAPPED
Copyright © 2013 by Clifford B. Bowyer

Cover Photograph by Susan Marie Photography

First printing September 2013
10 9 8 7 6 5 4 3 2 1

ISBN # 1-60975-075-6
ISBN-13 # 978-1-60975-075-6
LCCN # 2013910559

Silver Leaf Books, LLC
P.O. Box 6460
Holliston, MA 01746
+1-888-823-6450

Visit our web site at www.SilverLeafBooks.com

In loving memory of my sister, Linda Karner. She had always been one of the strongest people I know, always finding the bright side of every situation and fighting to make the most of each and every moment. She was an inspiration that I can only hope I am worthy enough to live up to. I love you and miss you dearly.

SNAPPED

PROLOGUE

"Dig it! Dig it! Dig it!"

He loved this. He felt so alive. Alex paddled as hard as he could through the white rapids as they headed for a class four drop. Their guide was screaming on the top of his lungs for them to keep paddling—to dig it—so that they would hit the rapid just perfectly. As the water poured over the boat, soaking them all, he felt a sense of exhilaration, as if truly alive.

"Yeah-ha-ha!" Alex screamed as they came out of the drop. In the seat next to him his father held his left fist out and they knocked hands together. "That was awesome!"

"There's more to come," his father said, lifting his chin to show the rough rapids ahead.

"Let's get 'em!" Alex cheered.

The tour guide—Dickie—agreed completely. "Everyone got one more in them? Good! Then let's Dig it! Dig it! Dig it!"

Alex began paddling harder again, pushing as hard as his twelve-year-old muscles would let him. He spotted someone with a camera on the side of the river taking pictures. He grinned knowingly—this would be the souvenir shot. He wanted to make it extra special. He showed his teeth, smiling as wide as he could while still paddling as hard as he could as they hit the rapid. The water got into his mouth and he began coughing, but he did not care—he was sure the picture got him with a smile on.

As they came out of the wave Alex looked ahead and saw that the river was slowing down. There was still white water, but they had gone through the roughest of the rapids already. He frowned, not wanting it to be over. They had paid extra for a big rapid day and certainly were not disappointed, but he wished it had lasted longer than it had.

From the seat behind him his mother leaned forward and pulled him into a hug. "Did you have fun?"

"You know I did," Alex said.

"Good. You were paddling really hard. Hope you worked up an appetite. We'll be stopping soon."

"I can eat," Alex said. Alex could always eat, and ate anything set down in front of him. He savored every last bite and loved the fact that he never gained weight regardless of what he shoved into his mouth.

He had enjoyed the river, especially on a big water day. This was not their first time white water rafting, but it was definitely the biggest rapids they had seen thus far. Alex's family, the Adams, were what he liked to consider adrenaline-junkies. They always picked their vacations doing things that most people would balk at. The bigger the thrill the more they liked it. He may only be twelve, but he had already been mountain climbing, base jumping, hang gliding, parachuting—no feeling in the world like jumping out of a perfectly good airplane—scuba diving with sharks, and rafting. They had almost gone skiing this year instead of the rafting trip, but Alex was glad they came here. He preferred the warmth to the icy climates, but still looked forward to skiing some weekend in the winter.

His father, Andrew—Andy—Adams was a magazine writer who wrote articles and reviews of vacation destinations. His articles were always the ones that depicted the more dangerous outings—someone else could write about sitting out on a beach; that was not what the Adams were all about. In addition to writing, he was an avid sports enthusiast who always saw something and wanted to try it—and strive to be better at it than the person he saw doing it.

Alex really looked up to his father—idolized him, even. He never did anything in life where he did not push to be the best. Second place was only the first-place-loser in his eyes. But he would not know—he always came in first for everything he did. He had a room full of trophies, and awards to prove it, from soccer to baseball to pop-warner football to archery to shooting matches and even academics. He had a thirst for success—never wanting to let his parents down and feel disappointment in him—and thrived on being the best.

His mother, Alicia Adams was a veterinarian. But she did not just treat animals at a local clinic; she went around the world to help wild life in their natural environment—or at least she had before she got married. Once she and Andy met her trips slowed down, and she stayed more local. Still, she had a heart of solid gold and felt that the slightest injury to any animal was a great injustice.

Alex learned his compassion from his mother. Her tenderness, her caring attitude, and her belief in how sacred all life was. He would not even kill a spider in his room; instead he carefully coaxed it to step onto a piece of paper and then slowly made his way to the door to let it outside. He also saw how protective she was of the things she loved and cared about, and he did as well. He actively stood between the bullies at school and the kids that they picked on. Very few bullies were actually brave enough to confront him and they all backed down quickly. At least they did if they knew what was good for them.

As for Alex, he could not imagine a more ideal life. He saw so much tragedy and darkness in the world, but felt none of it personally. He had never seen his parents argue, and lived in a world full of warmth, love, and excitement. Half of his friends were from broken homes where their parents had been divorced. Alex could never imagine his parents separating—and hoped that the day he finally got married that it would be the perfect person to complete him, like his parents completed each other, and that they would be happy for all eternity. But he had a few years before he had to worry about that.

Dickie had their raft—a group that included his family and five others—pull over to the left and come to a stop. "Very good, everyone. We really hit those rapids perfectly."

"Yeah we did," Alex's father said, hitting Alex's fist again.

"I need three volunteers," Dickie said as he walked to the edge of the raft and jumped off.

"I'm in," Alex said.

"Me too," his father replied.

Another boy in the back came out, too, but not because he wanted to. His father had to coax him, ask him, "Why don't you go?" Alex looked at him and rolled his eyes. The boy did not even look like he was enjoying himself. How can you not enjoy this? This was nature at its best. This was the fury of river and man trying to conquer it. At any moment someone could fall overboard and never be seen again. It did not matter that they all wore helmets and life jackets—the river was a deadly place if one did not respect it.

"All right then, let's go," Dickie said. He led them up a trail that had logs for stairs that seemed to go on forever. It was nothing compared to the Nutcracker at Yosemite Valley that they climbed, and Alex and his father quickly took the lead as they ascended. Dickie told them to keep going all the way to the top—even as a rafting guide, he was not nearly in the same shape that they were. The other boy stayed a few steps behind Dickie.

At the top there was someone else from base camp who was there with buckets, bags, and other supplies. Dickie arrived and told everyone to take one of the buckets back down. He picked up a large red bag and hefted it over his shoulder. Alex lifted up one of the buckets—it was fairly heavy, but manageable.

They then went back down the stairs for the raft. Alex and his father arrived first again and stood on the rocks without getting into the raft. Both held their buckets without putting them down. Alex glanced up to see the progress of Dickie and the other boy and snorted when he saw the other boy putting his bucket down on the steps and resting. Some people just did not have what it took to be athletic and adventurous.

The two arrived and Dickie had them hand the buckets into the raft and put them in the middle. He explained that the supplies they got would all be taken out a bit further down the river for lunch. He then got into the raft and helped the others back in. Alex did not need help. He got in just fine.

The raft remained where it was while the rest of the rafts from the same tour group all joined them. They had about a dozen groups in all—the rafts from this particular tour were all either purple or turquoise.

"So where is everyone from?" Dickie asked while they waited.

"Baltimore," one man said for him and the woman he was with.

"We're from New Hampshire," the father of the boy who went up to get supplies with them added.

"Massachusetts," Alex's father said. "About thirty minutes west of Boston."

"How do you like the river?" Dickie asked.

"It's great," the Baltimore woman said. "This is so much fun."

"It's a nice day for it, too," Dickie said. "There has been a lot of rain of late. But no rain today. That means more water in the river for better rapids and a crystal clear day to enjoy it."

"The weather is definitely amazing," Alex's mother said.

"Will we hit any more rapids?" Alex asked.

"Part of the river picks up again pretty good," Dickie said. "But the big stuff is all behind us. We'll hit that on the way to the camp site and then it's smooth the rest of the way."

Alex frowned. He wanted more excitement. How fun was it sitting in a raft and just drifting? He did not want a tan, he wanted the thrill.

His father patted his helmet. "It'll be nice and relaxing.

Enjoy it."

"I guess," Alex said, but he was not convinced. He doubted his father was sincere either.

"I can't wait to be off this stupid river," the boy said.

Alex turned and stared at him, shocked. Did he really not like this?

"You're not having fun, Jimmy?"

"I just want to go."

"Well, raftings not for everyone," Dickie said with a shrug. He then looked at the other boats and nodded. "We can set off now." He got out of the raft and pushed it back into the river, hopping back in. As he sat down another one of the tour guides used his paddle to splash water at Dickie. Dickie laughed, "This means war! Get 'em!"

Alex did not need to be told twice. He plunged his paddle in the water and began splashing the other boat. Both boats began doing it, soaking each other. The cool water felt good after just sitting there in the sun for so long.

"Okay, we're off," Dickie said as the current caught them and they began heading down river again, leaving the other raft behind them with people shouting that they would catch up later.

They did pick up pace as Dickie promised, but the river was just fast. There were no big dips, cascading waters, or thrilling moments. Before they knew it they were at the campsite. They were able to take off their helmets and life jackets for the first time and left the raft for land where the tour guides all got together and created a food station. The tour guides also pointed out the bathrooms if needed—up the hill and out of site, wherever people felt comfortable.

When the tour guides were ready they called people up by raft. Dickie's was the third raft called. Lunch had the offerings of a salad and a wrap. The wrap had turkey, some more lettuce and other things to add in, and some "special sauce." For desert there were cookies. There were also mugs of hot chocolate for those who were cold by the river, or cups of soda, juice, or water.

Alex hesitated with the salad but took it—he did not really want it but did not think the wrap alone would be enough food. For the wrap he had them put everything in it to make it as thick as possible. He also grabbed a cookie and decided on a soda rather than the hot chocolate—which just seemed to go better with a salad and wrap.

The tour guides also began a fire; there were logs around it to sit. Alex did not need to sit by the fire—he was not cold in the least. He found another log that was further away from people and his parents joined him there. The three of them ate, talked about the rapids and the river thus far, and laughed at each other's jokes. It was the kind of adventure that he knew he would always remember and cherish. These were the moments that kids captured. The moments that stayed with them forever.

After lunch was done his father walked up the hill to go to the bathroom. He had asked Alex if he wanted to come, but Alex said no. Before everyone was almost done eating though, his father suggested that he really better go because there would not be another stop until they got back to base camp. Alex reluctantly agreed to go.

He walked up the hill and kept going. At least if he was up here he might as well explore a little and see what he could come up with. Beyond the hill he found a large drop off onto rocks below. There was some water, but not much. He peered over the edge and wondered if he had time to climb down and back up it, but decided against it. He did not want to worry his parents or cause a scene. As he turned around the other boy was there—Jimmy.

"What'cha doin'?"

"Just exploring," Alex said. The attitude Jimmy was giving all day he wondered if something as simple as exploring would even register to the boy.

"You really like all of this, don't you?" Jimmy asked.

"I love it," Alex said.

"Whatever," Jimmy replied. As he turned away from Alex he saw something that caught his attention. He reached down, picked up a rock, and threw it.

Alex watched and then his eyes grew as he saw the rock strike a hawk that was resting in a nest.

"Got it!" Jimmy cheered, pumping his fist as the hawk

fell out of the nest.

"What the hell did you do that for?" Alex demanded.

"Because I could," Jimmy said. He then ran to the branch stretched out over the ravine where the nest was and hesitantly crawled out on it.

"What are you doing?" Alex demanded again, wondering how a kid who found rafting boring could crawl out on the limb of a tree over a ravine. If Jimmy was not an adventurous soul, why do this?

"Chicken," Jimmy said with a glare that told Alex just what he thought about him.

"I'm not chicken, I just don't know what you're game is."

"There's a nest," Jimmy said. "I'm gonna see what's in it!"

Alex shifted his gaze from Jimmy to the nest he was crawling toward. He then peered over to see the hawk that had fallen below. His eyes narrowed, threateningly. "Don't even think about it. It's bad enough what you did to the mother."

"What do I care? They're just stupid birds."

"What did they ever do to you?" Alex asked.

"They existed," Jimmy said. He reached out into the nest and lifted an egg. "There is one!"

"Leave it alone!" Alex shouted.

"Why don't you come out here and make me?" Jimmy

sneered. He stared at Alex, holding the egg, and then laughed. "That's what I thought."

"Just put it down," Alex said. "Gently."

"Sure, of course," Jimmy said. But he did not put it down. He squeezed the egg and it burst, killing the baby hawk inside.

"No!" Alex screamed. "You monster!"

Jimmy laughed hysterically. Alex could not believe his cruelty. How could he take the life of something so innocent, so precious, and just laugh about it? He ran for the branch before he even knew what he was doing and pushed as hard as he could. The branch shook, and Jimmy held on for dear life.

"What the hell are you doing?" Jimmy demanded, now looking scared for the first time.

Alex did not answer, he just kept pushing at the branch.

Jimmy held on, but the shaking branch began tipping, further lodged from the edge. It was amazing that the fallen tree had been so sturdy under Jimmy's weight, but with Alex pushing, gravity was about to prove its superiority.

"Don't, I'll fall!" Jimmy said.

"Did you give the hawk a chance?" Alex asked as he pushed again.

"Please!" Jimmy pleaded.

Alex stopped. He did not want to be as bad as this boy. Perhaps Jimmy had learned his lesson. Perhaps he had some sense knocked into him. Perhaps he would never harm another animal again. He stepped back so that Jimmy could get back up.

"It's still falling," Jimmy said. "Give me your hand!"

Alex frowned. He could not believe he was saving the cruel boy. But he held his hand out and let Jimmy clasp it. He then pulled him forward and as the branch gave way and fell into the ravine below, Alex held Jimmy tightly, just as tightly as he was trained to hold someone on a mountain if they lost their grip. There was no way Jimmy would fall. Alex knew what he was doing and let his training take over.

"Don't drop me!" Jimmy pleaded.

Alex pulled him up. "Wuus."

Jimmy shoved him. "What the hell did you do that for? I could have died!"

"You deserved it for what you did," Alex said. "Hopefully now you'll know how precious all life is."

"Yeah, whatever," Jimmy said.

Alex's eyes opened wide. Jimmy had not learned a thing. He growled as he charged Jimmy, and as Jimmy turned around, looking confused, Alex pushed and watched Jimmy fall over the edge and land on the rocks below, ironically lying right next to the hawk he had killed.

Alex stared down at Jimmy, the boy's eyes lifelessly looking up at him, a pool of blood beginning to trickle down beneath his head, his back, and pool out over the rocks beneath him. Alex had never seen somebody die before, but as he stared down at Jimmy's body, he did not feel anything of what he had expected to feel. The one thing he most definitely was not was sorry. Jimmy got what he deserved. All life was important. Those who would so carelessly take it away deserved what they got.

He wondered, briefly, if he deserved the same fate for what he had just done. But he brushed it off. There was a major difference between him—someone who was avenging a senseless murder—and Jimmy—a boy who took like and made a joke out of it. No, Alex realized he did not deserve the same fate. He was justified in what he had done. He spared the world any number of cruel injustices that Jimmy could have unleashed upon it. How many lives he had saved. He had done the right thing.

Alex headed back to the camp and made his way to his parents.

"Were you able to go?" his father asked.

"I did some exploring," Alex shrugged. "I really didn't have to go."

"Don't come complaining to me if you have to go before we get back."

"I won't," Alex said. "So when are we heading out?"

"Soon I think," he said.

The tour guides walked around telling everyone to head back to their rafts if they were done. Dickie stood by theirs and greeted them. "How was lunch?"

"Everything was delicious," Alex said, nodding enthusiastically. "I could have had more though."

"You always could have more," his mother teased as she got back in the raft and began putting her gear back on. Alex and his father did the same. The couple from Baltimore also got in and got ready to go. The couple from New Hampshire—Jimmy's parents—was looking up the hill trying to find him.

"Has anyone seen Jimmy?" the mother asked.

Dickie looked out over the camp for the boy but did not see him. "Did he wander off? When did you see him last?"

"He went to go to the bathroom," Jimmy's mother said.

"I'll go find him," the father replied.

"Need some help?" Alex's father asked.

"I'd appreciate that," the man said.

"Hold on, I'll get the tour guides to help out too," Dickie added. Within minutes there were twelve tour guides and about twenty volunteers—including Alex—looking for the lost boy.

"I hope he didn't wander too far back," Dickie said. "There's a big drop off back there. It could be dangerous."

"Oh my God," the father said. "Jimmy! Jimmy!"

Alex heard shouts for Jimmy from all around. He joined in as well calling the name of the boy. He knew right where to go, but leading the group there would not be in his best interests. After all, how come he knew where Jimmy had fallen?

"Up there is where the drop off is," Dickie said. Several people broke off to go look, including a few of the tour guides. Alex could tell just by looking at them that they were afraid that they were about to find the boy right where they should not.

"I'll look over here," Dickie said. He stepped up to the edge, froze in place, and then turned quickly and grabbed Jimmy's father, pulling him away. "You don't want to see this. Trust me."

"Jimmy? You found my boy? Jimmy! Jimmy!"

The other tour guides gathered around and looked. Alex stepped up to the ledge and looked over, too, seeing Jimmy right where he had fallen, still staring up lifelessly. He then glanced at Jimmy's father and felt the first stab of guilt. He wished the man, and inevitably his wife, would not have been hurt. But maybe they were better off without Jimmy, too. Perhaps Jimmy learned his cruelty from them. Perhaps their suffering was also deserved. Regardless, he was not sorry for the boy, but for the pain they were going through.

Alex's father took him by the shoulder and guided him away from the ledge. "You shouldn't have to see this," he said. Alex let his father bring him away, knowing how concerned he was that Alex would have nightmares or be scared by this experience.

As his father led him further away Alex heard the tour guides talking.

"He must have gotten too close to the ledge."

"Looks like he knocked the tree out. Maybe he saw the nest and was trying to see if there were eggs."

"Poor kid."

An accident. They thought it was an accident. Alex pondered that for a moment. He would not get in trouble for this. They would get the rest of the way down river and go about their lives. He wondered if Jimmy's lifeless eyes would haunt him or if he could put this behind him. He thought about the bird Jimmy struck with the rock and then the egg he so maliciously crushed. No, he would not be haunted. He would sleep soundly with no regret or remorse at all.

1

The wail of the alarm clock woke them. Alex leaned over, clicking it off and then turned back and kissed his wife's forehead. "Rise and shine."

She groaned and buried her head in her pillow. "Remind me why we have to get up so early again?"

"To go back to school and tell them all about how wonderful life can be after graduation," Alex said.

"You mean to lie to them and fill their heads with fantasy?"

Alex laughed, "You're going to be a cheery presenter today." He then reached down and tickled her. She squirmed; protesting at him doing it, but then began giggling.

"Okay, okay, I'm up, I'm up," she said.

"You sure?" he asked as he moved his fingers quickly

and tickled her some more.

"I'm sure, I'm sure!" she squealed.

"Good," Alex said, kissing her forehead again. "We can't disappoint the kids."

She sat up leaning on her elbow. "You know, they're just excited not to have to be in class, and really, are going to be bored out of their minds, right?"

"Maybe for *your* presentation," Alex grinned. "They'll love mine."

"You just keep telling yourself that," she said. "Do you want coffee first or to hop in the shower?"

"I'll take my shower," Alex said. "I'll be quick."

"Okay, I'll go make the coffee."

Alex watched her get up from bed and walk to the door-way. She glanced back and caught him admiring her. Even after ten years of marriage, she could see how much he loved her and admired her just by the way he looked at her.

Alex had really struck gold in life. He had married his High School sweetheart—none other than head cheer-leader, Crystal Cummings, only the most gorgeous girl who ever set foot in the town of Hopkinton, Massachusetts. He went to college at MIT, and then got a graduate degree in business from Harvard. The entire world was open to him, and he found something that he adored—video games. Who said someone who grew up could not enjoy what they did for a living?

He often considered his former classmates who went

into various professions. How they sat at a computer all day typing away, or entering trades, or writing reports, or trying to create advertising, or doing sales. He could have done any of that or more, but the most thrilling thing to him was finding the latest technology, pushing things to the limit, and being the man behind the success of a new launch. The sales and online subscribers were his indicator of success, and some of his games were amongst the most popular currently on the market.

A beautiful wife, and a career where he got to think up and play games for a living—he could not think of anything that would make things better. Well, there was always a child to call their own, but they still had time for that. Right now they got to enjoy their lives, enjoy their vacations, and enjoy each other. Besides, his wife was not just the head cheerleader—she was a supermodel. How many men got to go home every night to the woman other men fantasized about?

Between them, they had enough money to buy a house in Wellesley that was considerably larger and fancier than their needs. But it was home and they loved it. It was a symbol of their status and achievements—and by entering the new community, a blaring call sign that they belonged in Wellesley. Not that Alex cared about what others thought of him, but one day his kids would be in the school system and he knew how cliques and the old guard could cause some issues along the way.

They both also drove a Mercedes, which seemed to be a fairly common vehicle in their neighborhood—that or a Lexus, Cadillac, or Audi. Alex went with the sports utility vehicle—the GL450 SUV with a metallic obsidian black exterior and an ash leather interior. Crystal preferred the more sporty look and had a convertible—the SLR McLaren Roadster with a metallic storm red exterior, black soft top, and stone leather interior. For their weekend getaways and excursions they also had a Jeep Rubicon with a natural green pearl exterior and a gray slate interior. On all three they had spared no expense in getting the options and added features. They both loved their cars, and everything that they symbolized.

Alex had thought long and hard about hybrids and finding something that would be more environmentally friendly. He had not gone completely green, as the buzz word may be, but he paid his bills online without getting any statements or paper invoices, he used the recycled bags for food shopping, he refilled water bottles instead of throwing them away, and donated money every year to help protect the wild life and nature preserves. But when it came to his cars, he just did not like the look and style of the hybrids and decided that he and Crystal could be afforded at least one luxury with everything else that they did.

Maybe two luxuries—they owned a fifty-foot sailboat, too. But at least it was a sailboat, and not a motorboat. A little more work, but he loved it. They could sail for hours, or even days, if they had the time. Crystal had been really busy with her photo shoots as of late. She had been flying all over the world for magazine covers and images that her agent wanted her in. It had been too long since they just got on the boat and sailed together. He decided that he would try to find some time for them both to get away for a while.

When Alex was done with his shower and finished up in the bathroom, Crystal had his mug of coffee waiting for him. He savored the sweet aroma of the coffee and then took a sip. It was simply divine. She always knew how to make a good cup of coffee.

She slipped past him and went into the bathroom as he made his way to the walk-in closet to figure out what to wear. He decided to stick with his signature color—black—and went with a black suit, electric blue shirt, and a black and blue tie. Everything was crisp, clean, and screamed at success.

Crystal went with black, too. A one-piece dress that went to her knees, high heals, a bracelet, necklace, and earrings—all of which were accentuated by diamonds. Even getting ready for this simple event he could not help but think that she looked like she was ready for a photo shoot.

Alex drove, taking the SUV. From Wellesley to Hopkinton he went route 9 most of the way and then down 135 into down town and to the High School. The entire trip took under half an hour. As he pulled to a stop he glanced at the readout. They were right on time.

"You ready?" Alex asked.

"Always," Crystal said.

He got out of the car, walked around, and opened her door for her. Crystal stepped out and shook her hair just right so it would flow and land over her shoulders. It looked staged, but she always did it when getting out of a vehicle. Alex then reached into the back seat and pulled out a small bag that he brought as a surprise for the kids.

After closing the door and locking the car Alex took Crystal's hand and walked in through the front doors of the school they had both once attended and had considered their own. This was more than just an invite to speak to the kids—this was like coming home for them. She was the head cheerleader and the lead in almost every play. He was the star quarterback who doubled as valedictorian. They were teen royalty when they were here. Everyone loved them and wanted to be them. That was a desire that never went away. Alex always caught looks of envy when people saw he and Crystal together.

A table was set up inside and several people were sitting there. "Good morning, are you here to speak to the students?"

"We are," Alex said.

"What's your names?"

"Alexander and Crystal Adams," Alex said.

A head turned behind the table and Alex saw one of the women smile. "Alexander Adams and Crystal Cummings!

What a pleasure to have you both back!"

Alex recognized her at once. Principal Davies had first taken the job during their sophomore year. She had been one of the people who wrote Alex's recommendation to MIT for him. "Principal Davies," Alex said with a slight bow and smile.

"Oh rubbish. We're all adults now. It's Rhonda."

Alex took Rhonda's hand and kissed the back of it. "Rhonda, if you wish."

"Crystal, you have to keep your eye on this one," Rhonda said. "Such a charmer."

"He is that," Crystal said, pulling Alex a little closer to her. "I keep an eye on him though."

One of the women at the table held out a folder for each of them with their names on it. "Your assignments and the schedule are in your respective folders."

Alex opened his up and glanced down at the itinerary. They were beginning in the cafeteria where refreshments were being served, then moving into the gym where the student body would be waiting—Alex looked forward to seeing the gym again. He had a lot of memories in there. After the opening ceremonies they all went to various classrooms where smaller groups of the senior class students would come in and meet them.

"Room 220," Alex said.

"115," Crystal replied.

"So far apart," Alex sighed. "I don't know if we can bare

it."

Principal Davies laughed. "You two are so cute together."

"Thanks," Alex said.

"I'll see you in the gym, I'm sure," she said.

Alex and Crystal headed for the cafeteria and poked their heads in. They both took a small pastry and bottled water while they were waiting.

"Think we could still get into our old lockers?" he asked.

"You remember your combination?"

"Don't you?"

"I don't even remember where it was," Crystal shrugged.

"Don't worry, I know where yours was," Alex replied with a wink. "Maybe we'll check them on the way out."

"They're not ours anymore," Crystal said.

"They should be," Alex frowned. "You'd think they would have at least had them bronzed or something for us."

"Only you," Crystal said as she nudged his shoulder, teasingly.

"Let's head over to the gym," Alex suggested. Crystal nodded in agreement and they made their way down to the gymnasium. When the school was rebuilt the town decided to make an exception gym rather than the auditorium. A lot of functions and things like the school plays were done in the Middle School instead rather than the High School.

Alex and Crystal walked in to the gym—a temple for both of them—and looked around. It looked like graduation had with seats on rises for the guest speakers, giant screens that showed whoever was at the podium, and the bleachers rolled out for the students. Both walked in, admired their surroundings, and took a seat near the podium.

The bell rang and there was an announcement for all seniors and guest speakers to make their way to the gymnasium. Alex and Crystal watched as first a few curious faces stepped in, and then large crowds as the seats began filling up.

Principal Davies made her way to the podium and waited for the bell to ring again. Alex glanced up and saw her on the two screens above so that no matter where someone sat they could see her. It was impressive how a High School was able to afford such a system. The boosters had to be exceptionally generous the year this was all designed.

"Good morning," Principal Davies began. She then spoke about how exciting the future was, and how many opportunities awaited the students in the months and years to come. She also thanked all of the guest speakers who took time out of their busy days to come and speak to the students about what they do and to spend time with the kids. When she was done a father of one of the students got up to speak. He had begun his own company and grew it into an online giant with nearly a billion hits a day. His message was optimistic, positive, and sent the kids off think-ing that hard work and determination could let them achieve their dreams. Alex liked the message. It was a good one.

When the bell rang for the next period Alex hugged Crystal and wished her luck with her presentation. He then made his way to room 220 and sat down on the radiator in back. There were two other presenters in the room already and he quickly kicked off introductions and getting them talking to each other. It was all in the approach—charisma. It never took much for Alex to get people talking.

Usually with presentations he liked to set the pace and go first. But he was curious about what the others did for a living and expected that making video games would be a big winner. He wanted to see how the kids responded to the speeches and then try to wow them—then he could tell Crystal for certain that they were genuinely interested in what he had to say.

"Who wants to go first?" Alex asked.

"Doesn't matter," the guy said.

"I don't care," the woman said.

"Well, ladies first then," Alex said, extending his arm to prompt her to speak.

She went up, introduced herself, and then began talking about what she did. She worked in marketing and created advertising for major corporations. Alex listened to her and examined the crowd as she talked about how you gain an account, study the client needs, and then work on brain-storming to find the right ideas to pitch the client. She had a few poster-boards to show an example of a current campaign she was working on. When she was done she fielded questions and then came back to the radiator.

"You're up," Alex said pleasantly. The other presenter nodded and went to the front. He was a photographer and pulled out a laptop to show some of his shots. He had been all around the world to capture some amazing sights. Alex admired quite a few pictures and could relate to how difficult it would be to reach the points where he was to take the shot. A fellow adventurer. A kindred spirit.

After the photographer was done, Alex took his bag and walked to the front of the room. "Wow, those were both fascinating. Let's give our presenters a round of applause, shall we?" he said. The class clapped and he saw the two fellow presenters looking pleased. He was glad. Both were quite good with their discussions, clearly passionate about their work, and had taken time to try and share that excitement and love for what they did with others. It was nice for the kids to acknowledge that, and he was glad to do his part to get them that recognition.

Alex handed a stack of index cards to the students in the front row. "Pass those back," he said. "If everyone could put their name on the index card and then pass them up to your teacher when done."

The teacher was sitting at his desk and nodded. Alex

then continued.

"Well, good morning all. I'm Alexander Adams, and it wasn't all that long ago that I was sitting in those very same desks as you, listening to someone else trying to tell me what the real world was all about. I remember thinking about how I would do better than the people I heard speaking. At how their words of caution about expectations and reality just brushed off of me. I wouldn't fall for that. I would be a success and there was no doubt about it.

"I also remember how people spoke about how your upbringing, your education can really make or break you, and how being a product of this town and this school has really given you all an advantage. I can honestly say, that is very true.

"I believe that there is a fine line between cockiness and confidence, but with the education I gained here, I have learned to walk that line. I can't tell you how many people I have seen in college, in graduate school, in the business world who had come from different worlds and struggled.

"I took a writing class in college and thought it was the biggest breeze in the world. No matter what I did or how much effort I put into it I always got an A. I thought the professor was just really easy, so I recommended him to my roommate. My roommate could never get higher than a C. I tried to help, but after reading, I just didn't have the patience to try and teach him that which those of us who went to Hopkinton already know so well.

"It's really a testament to the teachers here, the parents and boosters who take so much pride in the school, and all of the students who thrive in this system. We're not just successful because we want to be, we thrive because this is what we were brought up to do. We don't have a choice, really. We're already the elite. We already know more than most of the people who will be our peers."

Alex looked around the room and shrugged. "Guess you can see what side of walking that line between cockiness and confidence I tend to lean toward, right?" he was glad that there were some laughs from the students. They were actually listening. He liked that.

"So what brings me here today?" Alex asked. "Today I'm here to tell you about what I do. So what is that? It's quite simply, actually. I'm what is called a Project Manager."

Alex paused again, looking around at the faces of the students. "I know, I know. A Project Manager. Whoop-de-do. How exciting? But a Project Manager is really the one who is behind a lot of advancements. I've always been of the belief that I don't need to know anything about what I'm running, as long as I know how to run a project, organize things, and motivate people. Does everyone follow that?"

He saw some blank expressions and decided to clarify. "Let's say for example that I was a Project Manager in a financial institution. Maybe, there's some kind of development that needs to be done to meet the needs of a client. Do I need to know what investments they are doing? No. There are financial brokers for that. Do I need to know how the technology will work? No. There are developers and IT people for that. Do I need to know how to test it to make sure it works? No. There are quality assurance people for that. So what do I need to know how to do?"

Alex paused for dramatic effect. "Quite simply, I need to know how to keep all of those people working effectively, together, and to meet the common goal and deadline. I don't care what a developer is doing, as long as they are doing it. Does that make sense?"

Alex looked around again and saw some nods. "What if I was a Project Manager working for the airlines? Do I need to be an engineer and able to pull a plane apart and rebuild it? No. I just need to make sure the engineer is doing what I need them to do. Regardless of what industry you are in, there is always a need for the people who know how to facilitate projects and make things happen.

"I bet you're wondering what I really do, right?" Alex asked and then laughed to himself. "Well, I make video games."

That got a reaction. He saw students sit up a little more straight in their chairs. Some smiled. One even cheered.

"I have a team of people who work for me. I have analysts who go over the market and potential games to see what would be good for the market. I have concept people who look at options, features, and things that we could incorporate into the game. I have concept artists who sketch out the things we're building so the designers can take it from there. I have designers who code and actually make the game. I have testers who playtest, and make sure the game is fun, challenging—but not overly difficult—and is free of glitches and defects; things we call bugs. Then there are the marketing people who work with us to make sure they capture the essence of the game we're designing for when they bring it to market."

Alex raised his arms and beckoned the class. "Instead of talking more about what I do, how about some questions? I'd be happy to answer anything you have."

He got the questions he pretty much expected. They wanted to know what kind of games he made, had they ever heard of them, and did he play games himself? What kind of education did you need to do what he did? Was there good money in it? Did he ever have a game that flopped? Alex answered each question clearly and with conviction. The enthusiasm of the class was infectious and he easily spent more time at the front of the room than anyone else.

He glanced at the clock on the wall and saw that they were almost out of time. "Before we run out of time, I have a little drawing," Alex said. He took the index cards with student names on them, shuffled them, kept the names pointed toward himself, and then faced the class. "Can I have a volunteer please?"

One girl in the third row raised her hand. Alex asked her to take a card. She did and read off the name. Alex folded the cards back together and held his bag up. "Reach on in there and take something from inside."

The first boy who won reached in and came out with the disc for an online game—this one a fantasy adventure game about a Mage who conquered the Seven Kingdoms and the brave heroes having to try and reclaim the land.

"There's a code on the back that will let you play for free for a year," Alex said. He then fanned the index cards out again. "Another volunteer?"

He had a total of five winners and five give-away games. He wished everyone luck with their career paths and told them to have fun with the games. The bell rang, signaling the end of the first class. The way the schedule was set up the students rotated to rooms with guest speakers. Every student had the opportunity to go to three rooms, seeing three guest speakers in each. Alex did not know how it was determined which guest speakers they saw, but assumed that there had been some kind of questionnaire in advance so the kids saw speakers that catered to their interests.

The next class came in and the three presenters went through their routine again. By the time the third class came in, most of them were already aware that Alex worked for a gaming company and was giving away free samples in a drawing. The final class had been even more excited than the first.

When they were done they met in the cafeteria again where Alex found Crystal waiting for him—after, of course, stopping by his old locker and opening it on the first try. All presenters were all given Hopkinton sports bottles to thank them for coming and helping. Principal Davies went out of her way to find them and tell them that the kids could not stop talking about the game presentation and the handouts. She said that the free games were above and beyond what was expected and thanked him. Alex took it all in stride, said it was his pleasure, and then the Adams' left the school.

2

Creative Visions Entertainment—CVE—had originally been conceived of by a pair of avid video-gamers—Brett Curran and Daniel Greteman—who were disillusioned with Corporate America and wanted to put their education and passion to good use. Both were making good money, and leading good lives, but felt that there was more to life than what they had. After considering their options and thoroughly planning the launch of CVE, they resigned from their positions and put all of their money into their mutual dreams.

Their original idea was based on a flight simulator in space. It was fairly simple graphics, easy game controls, and one of the least expensive games they ever produced. It also was an instant success in the online gaming community—with people downloading the game and playing for hours. The flight simulator paved the way for a radical expansion, with even more bold and detailed games in the years to come.

Three years after they first began the new business they had an agreement in place for a console game. The agreement was a multi-million dollar deal and required the two entrepreneurs to think more about image, location, and employees. Working out of their home offices and via email had only gotten them so far.

They purchased a building in Worcester Massachusetts, keeping the costs lower than if they went closer to Boston, but also having enough space to handle the expansion and further growth that they anticipated the console deal would bring them. Thirty people were added to staff to work on the console game, creating the core of CVE.

Ten years later CVE has over three hundred employees and designs, and releases a dozen games a year, two or three of which usually are mainstream releases with hefty sales projections. Gamers may not know the CVE name, but they certainly recognize the titles of the games that are released.

Alex had joined CVE after completing his Masters at Harvard. He had the skills that the company was looking for—he enjoyed video games, he was able to come up with ideas and brainstorm things without taking so much pride in his idea that he got overbearing and stubborn, he had technical aptitude, he had a business degree that he knew how to lead and motivate with, and he had a positive attitude that was infectious.

Interviewing at CVE was a bit different than at other places. Instead of a few interviews with different people, there was a month-long activity and observation period where people interested were all brought into a conference room, given a mock-project and then left on their own. Human Resources would observe the behavior of the people, the way they actually acted in groups, and see what roles were defined. Those that they liked from their observations were then brought in to interview with managers of the skill set they thought the individual best matched.

In Alex's case, he had taken charge of the room, motivated people, facilitated the discussions, and kept everyone focused. After the mock-project was done he was introduced to Karen Talbott and Barney Aulenback. Karen ran one of two project teams that focused on Fantasy games, with a particular emphasis on online roleplaying games. Barney was the senior vice president who oversaw both Fantasy teams—or sister groups as he called them.

Alex had not gotten the best vibe from Karen originally. She did not ask many questions, get into a good back-and-forth dialogue, or even show much enthusiasm for what she was doing. She basically read him the job description, told him a little bit about what she did, and then asked him to talk a bit about the jobs he had while in college and between undergraduate and graduate school. Barney was a little more friendly, but he only had a handful of minutes to meet with Alex, and then made his apologies, as he had to go to a meeting. When Alex left he was sure he had not gotten the job and that the month he spent working the mock-project was a waste of time. He received a surprisingly generous offer that night.

After getting the job, he and Karen actually hit it off really well. He learned that they both had gone to MIT, and she was a fellow adventure enthusiast with plenty of stories of her own. They were even able to compare a few notes on things that they had both done.

Karen worked with Alex for the first couple of projects to show him the ropes and her expectations, but then she left him alone to do things his own way. Every time she asked if he had time to work on something, he immediately said to send it his way. Most project managers had two or three games tops that they were working on in various stages. He had fifteen that he was managing by the time his one year anniversary hit.

He gave Karen a weekly status update on where things were and how they were progressing. Beyond that she left him alone to form his own team and run it however he wanted. Any problems went to him to resolve. There was nothing he hated more than something going wrong and Karen knowing about it before he did—it was his project, his responsibility, and he would deal with issues to find the solutions.

When Alex built his team the first person he brought in was Elissa King. He had met Elissa while at MIT. She was not a student, but someone he met at a part time job—Subway—that he had taken to bring in a little extra cash on the side. He recognized in her a tremendous talent with much untapped potential. It was not that she could make a sub-sandwich better than anyone else, but her insightful and well thought out discussions and ideas about things.

After graduating from MIT and taking his first "real job," he brought Elissa with him. Ever since she had followed him wherever he went. She even became one of the bridesmaids for Crystal at their wedding. While professionally Alex was helping her out, mentoring her, and bringing her into better companies with every move he made, personally she had run into a string of bad luck. She got pregnant on the first date with one man, having a child with a father who decided it was in his best interests to stop working and move out of state to live with his sister to dodge child support payments. She became pregnant again by another man when her first child was three, though this time he had done the honorable thing and married her. Tragically, on the way to the hospital to see his newborn baby a truck crashed into his car and he died before he could see them. Now she is a single mother of two children from two different fathers.

What impressed Alex the most was how she had gone through both incidents and did not let it overwhelm her.

She was a survivor, a fighter, and she was determined to give her kids a better life and more than she ever had herself. Even though she did not have the educational background to work at CVE, Alex knew that she was more than capable to become his right hand and help him lead projects. He had full control over building his team either from within or without, and he brought her in. There was rarely a meeting he went to when Elissa was not by his side—unless of course he was double booked and he ran one while she ran the other.

From the business side, the other member of his team was an intern from India—Junador Rana. In his first week Karen had warned Alex about a few people who had reputations of being difficult or even downright impossible to work with. Ironically, Alex had found a way to make those people his best workers. While they were downright evasive, rude, and arrogant with most people, he was able to see things from their perspective, and related with them enough where they respected him and became incredibly loyal. Junador was one. Karen had said that Junador was on a very thin line from being let go because people did not like working with him. He asked too many questions, seemed to think he knew a better way of doing things, and often showed that he had no respect for the managers or chain of command.

Alex originally said to keep Junador around because there was so much that he knew that Alex did not at the time. Junador was virtually a walking encyclopedia of information and Alex soaked it all in early on. Alex also kept a close eye on him, trying to learn just what Junador was motivated by. In the end, Alex realized that Junador was a perfectionist. He wanted things to not just be right, but exact. He may ask questions and bother people by pestering them, but at the heart of it he was pushing to make sure that whatever he was working on had no mistakes, was fully researched, and entirely accurate. Alex could respect that. When Karen asked, "Can I let him go now?" Alex said no and that he wanted to keep Junador around.

Junador was his lead analyst. It was his job to examine potential projects, weigh the benefits, costs, and marketing potential. He ran studies, estimates, and reported on his findings. Once a project was underway he also drafted up the documentation, supporting materials, and took on more of an administrative role for Alex with all paperwork. Although Elissa also did a lot of that, Junador was given anything that required updates, tracking, and similar things. Elissa was given more oversight and control to speak in Alex's stead.

Another individual who was deemed difficult to work with was lead developer, Douglas Malone. Doug was a genius when it came to coding. He could take the design specs and then make the final output look so much better than anyone dreamed, with few bugs to the system and even a few hidden features that no one else had thought of. But to say he was not a people person was an understatement. Sitting in a conference room, to Doug, was the biggest waste of time in the world. Talking to someone about anything that did not relate to the games he was working on was a close second. Alex found that short meetings that got to the point and then ended, as well as keeping things strictly business was the best approach to working with Doug. He was even surprised from time to time when Doug would crack a rare joke—but only on the really good days.

Doug had a staff of his own—Steven Reed and Damien Crespo. The three were largely dubbed the Three Musketeers in the company and all had completely different outlooks and attitudes. Steven knew gaming and knew coding. When he spoke, people listened. He could also hear a pitch and come up with half a dozen approaches on the fly without batting an eye. The man really knew his work. Damien, on the other hand, was the comic of the group. He laughed, he joked, he ran the office fantasy football league, and he rarely took anything seriously—anything, that is, but his work. To say that he could see things outside of the box was an understatement. He often was the Devil's Advocate in the room to make people think of the down side of issues, and then came up with ideas that nobody had ever even considered but ultimately found agreeable.

Before a game made it into the hands of the Three Musketeers though, it first had to be conceived and designed. Sharon Lang was the concept designer. After Junador made a pitch she would flush it out, come out with a basic storyboard for the game and features that it would have. She worked along with Alex, Elissa, and Junador to document her ideas and brainstorm with the entire team to make the game even better. The concept artist, Garrett Mills also helped by sketching everything and anything that Sharon was thinking and bring her vision to life.

Once a game was completed—conceived, drafted, designed, and developed—it had to go through what would end up being the longest period of all—playtesting. Playtesting was important because a highly anticipated game was often already promoted and there was a tremendous push to get it to market. Testers had to resist the urgency and make sure that there were no glitches or problems with the game. They worked hand in hand with the developers for any problems they found and the Three Musketeers would then make coding changes to fix the glitch. Every fix required testing to begin anew to make sure the change did not impact something already tested.

Alex could not be happier with his lead tester, Everton Taylor. He had found Everton in London at a convention and was instantly impressed with the man, his confidence, and his thoroughness. So much so that Alex managed to convince Karen and Barney that Everton needed to be given an offer that he could not possibly refuse. In the end, the offer was quite lucrative and Everton came to the states to work for CVE.

Although Alex only met with Everton, the playtesting staff had a dozen people who worked for Everton. Some had been colleagues of Everton's in London, but most were interns from India. Everton shielded his group, taking responsibility for their findings and making sure any setbacks landed on his shoulders and not theirs. Alex respected and admired the man, and Everton did likewise in return.

The final member of Alex's team was Sabrina Stanley. A graduate of Bentley College she was the marketing guru of the bunch. She often was the silent attendee in meetings, watching the project come together and keeping her own records. As soon as the game was in testing she had a full marketing campaign already drafted and ready to be rolled out. Alex found her thorough, insightful, and one of the most optimistic and positive people he had ever met. That attitude went into her work, and everyone was always excited to see how their "baby"—because every project became the team's baby—was going to be handled.

Compared to other teams at CVE, Alex's was definitely overworked. His people consistently worked long days, rarely were found milling around and discussing the latest office gossip, and always had something that they needed to get to. Although this was part of Alex's aggressive nature to keep on taking more, not once had any member of his team complained. Like him, they thrived on the work and pushed to excel. Karen's faith was rewarded again and again as Alex's team prospered.

But as Alex arrived at work half way through the day the afternoon he had done his guest speaking at Hopkinton High School, the office was abuzz with speculation and rumor. Everywhere he looked people were hovered over desks whispering, chatting, and not working. Something was going on.

Trusting that Elissa would have her finger on the pulse, he set his jacket down and then walked over to her desk and leaned on it. "What's going on?"

"We got an announcement about an hour ago about a merger," Elissa said.

"A merger?" Alex asked, surprised that he had not even caught wind of it. "With who?"

"Takato Games in Japan," Elissa replied.

"Takato," Alex said, chuckling to himself. "I went to grad school with Sayuri Takato, the daughter of the CEO of Takato Games."

Elissa studied him for a moment. "I know that look. You're plotting something."

"Me? Never," Alex said. "I'll be right back."

"Oh yeah, you, not plotting anything," Elissa laughed and rolled her eyes as Alex walked away.

Alex never was one to stand with formalities of rank. He spoke to the division head and the janitor with the same amount of respect—he actually knew the janitor and security guard at the front door by name. So when he had news that CVE was merging with Takato, he did not hesitate to walking right into Barney's office without an appointment.

As he was walking through the door he knocked twice and Barney looked up.

"Alex, what can I do for you?" Barney asked, waving him in even though Alex was already in the office.

"I want in," Alex said.

"In?"

"The Takato merger," Alex said. "You'll need someone to manage it from the Fantasy perspective, and I want my team to be at the forefront."

Barney grimaced. "Alex, this is all very new. We don't know what's going to happen yet."

"Actually, we do," Alex said. "Takato will be bringing over their games and departments will be merging. We'll have a site here and in Japan. Some games will come to us, likely the online ones, and some will go to them, likely the console games. There will also be new projects. We'll develop online versions of their games and they'll develop console versions of our games. One big happy family. But there will be a conversion, a blending, a meeting of the two entities to become one. I want in."

"You seem awfully sure of yourself," Barney said.

"My team can handle it. I also know Sayuri Takato personally. I do believe she is the third highest ranked executive in her father's company."

Barney typed something into his computer quick and then nodded. "She is at that."

"We worked really well together. We will work really well together again."

"Don't you already have sixteen projects you're managing now?" Barney asked.

"Twenty-three, but that's beside the point," Alex argued. "My team is best positioned to successfully manage this merger for our area. I know it. You know it. You just have to green light it."

Alex heard another knock on the door and turned to see Karen standing there. "He's certainly not lacking in the confidence department."

"Isn't that why you hired me?" Alex asked.

"One of the reasons," Karen nodded. "Give it to him."

"But he already has twenty-three projects," Barney protested.

"I'll make sure nothing slides," Karen said. "If I have to move something to one of my other project managers I will."

Alex rolled his eyes at that so only Karen could see— they both knew he would never willingly give up a project, or, for that matter, ever have the need to give up a project.

"You really want this?" Barney asked.

"I do," Alex said.

"Then pack your bags. You're going to Tokyo."

3

Alex contacted Human Resources and had them make arrangements for four to fly to Japan and for accommodations once they arrived. He brought Doug Malone, Everton Taylor, and Elissa with him—for Elissa he also needed added arrangements to take care of her kids, but a couple of phone calls and Elissa got her sister to take care of them for while she was away.

He had debated bringing Elissa. She was the one person he trusted to keep the office running smoothly while he was away, especially with the added responsibility of her kids. But she was his closest aid—his second in command—and if he was going to Japan to meet their future, she earned the right to be there with him. Karen promised to look after the team while he was away, with Junador stepping up to take on more responsibility with the roles that Alex and Elissa usually held. Steven Reed covered for Doug. Everton still planned to run the playtester team from his blackberry.

Alex sent the three of them home to get ready for the trip, but stayed late himself to make sure everything was under control and he was not leaving a mess for Karen and Junador to clean up. Like Everton he planned on staying in touch with his team via blackberry from the air.

Their flight was leaving Logan at 6:00 in the morning, so he had to be there no later than 4:00 to take care of all of the pre-flight boarding checks and arrangements. They did have to stop at the San Francisco International Airport for a connector flight. According to what HR gave him, they were scheduled to arrive in California at 9:50 AM and then depart again at 11:17. They then would go the rest of the way to Tokyo, arriving at the Narita International Airport at 3:30 PM in what was the following day due to the time zones.

He was amazed that tickets could be scheduled so last minute for his team. He wondered just how much those last minute tickets cost them. But then again, he guessed a few pricey tickets to Japan were nothing to what kind of money the merger was bringing to the table.

A little after 8:00, he decided that he had done everything that he needed to to help Junador cover for him while he was away. He always ran a tight ship and there were very few issues at the moment, but he needed to make sure he dotted all of his I's and crossed all of his T's so that his absence did not cause a break in the process. But he had faith in his team and knew that they would be able to cover.

Alex got home and found dinner in the refrigerator waiting for him. Crystal left a note that she was called for a photo shoot in the Bahamas and had an early flight. She had turned in early. Alex wondered if their flights were close enough together to share a ride to Logan.

He heated his dinner in the microwave and sat down to enjoy a dish of chicken marsala over pasta and had a red wine with it. Dinner was quite good and when he was finished he was full. He doubted he would be able to fall asleep, but also did not want to wake Crystal by packing and moving things around in the bedroom.

He quietly made his way in and saw that she was asleep. He then walked into the walk-in closet and took three suits, six shirts, and six ties off the rack. He brought them out of the bedroom, careful to be quiet so as not to disturb her, and put them down on the couch. He took a pair of dress shoes and put them out as well—one black, one burgundy. He also grabbed sneakers for when he was not working out of the downstairs closet.

He went back up and attempted to go into the drawers. He slowly crept one open, wincing as the bureau sounded like it was grinding with the movement, and took out underwear, socks, a few tee-shirts for when he was not working, and khaki pants. He brought those down to the couch and set them with the rest of his things.

In the bathroom he had a travel-bag already prepared with an extra toothbrush, toothpaste, razor, cologne, deodorant, and some Q-tips. He took the razor out and figured with the new airline regulations he would just have to buy a disposable one in Japan. He then checked to make sure he had enough of everything else in the bag or if it needed to be replenished. Once he was satisfied he brought that down, too.

The suitcases themselves he was afraid would cause a bit of noise getting and decided he would do that when he woke up in the morning. But everything was ready to go. While downstairs he pulled a pair of novels from the shelf of books he had not read yet and picked up a collection of magazines—a variety between video games and vacation destinations.

Alex looked around, tried to think if he forgot anything, was pleased with the ensemble, and went up to go to bed. He set the alarm for 2:30 AM. He would not get much sleep, but some was better than none. He leaned over, kissed Crystal on the forehead, then turned over and went to sleep.

4

The alarm clock went off way too early. Alex lazily shut it off, but Crystal leapt out of bed and began running around as if she were incredibly late. Alex perched himself up and lazily watched her, amused. How she had so much energy this early in the morning was beyond him.

"What time is your flight?" he asked.

"6:30," she said.

"Want to share a ride?"

Crystal stopped and looked at him. "You're going some-place too?"

"6:00 flight to Tokyo," Alex said. "Big merger at work with Takato Games."

"And you're going to Japan?"

"I am," Alex said smugly.

"How did you pull that one off?"

"I walked into Barney's office and told him I was going."

"He gave in?"

"It's the Adams charm," Alex said with a wink.

"I know all about the Adams charm," Crystal chuckled. "How long will you be gone?"

"Barney didn't say. I'm taking four suits and shirts for six days. We'll see what happens."

"You're all packed?"

"I'm all organized," he clarified. "I didn't want to risk waking you by banging the suitcases around."

Crystal glanced at the clock. "We have to hurry."

"No time to come back to bed for a while?" he asked with a suggestive grin.

"You're awful," Crystal said. "We'll never make our flights."

"But at least we'll have something to think about on our flights."

Crystal looked at the clock again, bit her lower lip, shrugged, and then lunged back for the bed. They could be a little late. The airports policy of being so early was rather burdensome. As long as they made their respective flights.

Alex and Crystal had shared a cab to Logan airport, hugged and kissed each other goodbye, and then went their separate ways. Alex saw quite a few familiar faces waiting for the flight in addition to the three members of his team he was bringing with him. It looked like half the flight was reserved for CVE. Human Resources must have really been working overtime to make this happen.

Everyone was groggy being so early. The normal pleasantries were exchanged, but people really did not seem to want to talk. Alex couldn't blame them. He would not mind being back in bed either.

Anyone who has ever been on the flight to Japan knows how difficult it is. The flight is not only long, but the sun travels with you, so there never is any down time to actually sleep. Alex saw a few people with masks to help them sleep, but he stayed up the entire time. He figured he would try to go to sleep early after arriving in Tokyo and then see if he could reset his system and internal clock to sleep on Japan time.

Overall Alex could not complain. The flight went smoothly and the connector flight left on time. They even landed at the Narita International Airport on time. Even more miraculous, was the fact that he and his three team members all recovered their luggage without having to send word back to San Francisco that something was routed to the wrong destination. Not everyone on the flight was so lucky, but Alex only cared about his people.

As they approached customs, he spotted a familiar face in a power-black suit waiting for them—Sayuri Takato. When she saw him her eyes widened in shock. Obviously she did not know he worked for Creative Visions Entertainment.

"Adams-San!" she shouted and then bowed politely.

"None of that," Alex said as he held his arms out and hugged Sayuri. "We know each other too well Sayuri to fall on tradition."

"That is true, Alex," she said, though saying his name seemed to be a strain for her, as if she needed to remain formal.

The rest of the CVE people gathered around to see what was happening with Alex and the executive from Takato Games. Sayuri broke the hug and bowed to several people. "If you'll come this way I have already seen to it that you have all been cleared through customs."

She led them through customs and out to the street where a dozen black sports utility vehicles were parked and men in tuxedos waited. As they approached the men bowed and then opened the back doors to let people in. With the doors open they rushed ahead to help with the luggage and put it in the back of the trucks.

"Adams-San, you'll ride with me?" Sayuri asked.

"Only if you agree to call me Alex," Alex teased.

"Alex," she said and nodded. "Alex it is."

"Then we would be honored," Alex said.

Sayuri's driver held the door open and let Sayuri, Alex, and his team get in. They waited for everyone to be loaded into the trucks and then all drove off one-behind-another to the Takato Tower in the heart of Tokyo.

Sayuri tried to point out a few sites as they were driving by. Places and things she thought that they might be interested in if they had time away from the board room. Traffic was tight, but they moved more swiftly than Alex had expected and reached the Takato Tower heading underground into a parking garage. More men in tuxedos were waiting for them there and led them to the elevators.

Alex and his team, who were still with Sayuri went up with the first elevator. When it reached the top of the Tower—the ninetieth floor—Sayuri stepped aside to let them out where several others were standing and waiting.

Alex led his group forward. One man held out his business card to Alex with one hand. Alex took his out of a small leather case and held it up as well. They exchanged cards and studied them. Alex had gone over the proper protocol with Sayuri on the way over—he was to receive the card, study it, appreciate it, and only then put it away. He was then to bow to acknowledge receipt of the card and exchange honors. This particular card belonged to Koichi Takato, Sayuri's older brother and Chief Operating Officer of Takato Games.

Alex bowed as he had been tutored and saw Koichi do the same.

"It is an honor to have you here, Adams-San," Koichi said.

"The honor is all mine, Takato-San," Alex replied.

"Koichi, Adams-San and I met at Harvard."

Koichi looked from his sister to Alex and nodded. "A good omen when two people know each other and are co-incidentally brought together in business."

"Let us all hope that's true," Alex said with another bow. Behind him the elevator opened and another group of CVE employees stepped through.

"Yuzo, could you please bring out guests to the board room?" Koici said.

One of the men bowed twice in quick succession. "Right this way."

Alex and his team followed Yuzo into one of the largest and fanciest rooms they had ever seen. The table was immaculately designed with hand carvings in the woodwork, and lined with chairs that put those of CVE to shame. One wall was a waterfall, with water trickling down the wall into a fountain. Another wall was an aquarium with breathtaking fish swimming through. The wall opposite the waterfall had windows to overlook Tokyo. The final wall had screens for video conferencing.

"Impressive," Everton said as he looked out the window.

"Please, have seat," Yuzo said, gesturing toward the chairs.

Alex sat down and felt like he was in a seat of luxury. These were the kind of chairs that only senior executives were privileged enough to sit in, yet every chair in the room was like that and it was incredibly comfortable.

Gradually more people began filing into the room. One side of the conference room table was filling up with people from CVE. The other was reserved for the executives of Takato Games. When the final CVE employee was seated, a man in a dark blue suit stepped in, bowed, and then made his way to the end table. He could only have been Sayuri's father—CEO and founder of Takato games, Tomiro Takato.

Tomiro stood by his chair waiting until all of his people were in the room, and then sat down. As soon as he did so the rest of his executives did as well. A woman rolled in a cart with pots of tea and poured cups offering them to the people at the table. Tomiro did not say anything while she was providing everyone with their tea. She served him last and he said, "Thank you, Mayumi."

Tomiro took a sip of his tea and then set the cup down. "Welcome, friends, to Takato Games. These are exciting times we have before us. Changing times. Times when our two companies will play to our strengths and overcome our respective weaknesses."

Alex could not help but grin. He was glad he had boldly gone into Barney's office and asked to be a part of this. Sitting here, in this room, with these people, he was making history. Neither of their companies would ever be the same again, and he was there at the beginning to be a part of it.

Tomiro did not speak long. He began with his vision,

then spoke quickly and to the point. To delay any more than that would be a waste of productivity. Mayumi returned then and placed a folder with itinerary down in front of everyone. Alex flipped through it and saw various meetings scheduled, tours of the Takato Tower and various divisions of game design, and even social engagements.

Most of it, however, began early the following morning. The Takato's must have been sympathetic to the long flight and how tired everyone from CVE would be. Alex was anxious to get started, but also liked the idea of trying to get some sleep.

After the meeting they were brought back down to the waiting SUV's and driven to a western-style hotel to stay. While the accommodations were familiar to that of a hotel in the states, Alex was impressed with the overall size and elegance of the arrangements. It was a beautiful hotel.

He dialed Crystal, getting her voicemail, and left a message to let her know he had arrived and was okay. He then checked his messages on his laptop and sent a few correspondence to Junador for things that needed to be done back home.

Looking at his watch it was early. Not even 8:00 yet. But he had not slept in so long that it did not matter. He took off his clothes and dropped on the bed. Before long, his wake up call rang and it was a brand new day.

5

The next few days in Japan were busy ones. Tomiro Takato had not been kidding about taking the night to rest because there was a lot of work to be done. The days began early and ended late. Each day was filled with meetings, training seminars, observations of the Takato Games process, and even some hands-on-tinkering with the teams to see exactly what they were working on.

The second night there had also been a formal dinner where all of the executives went to get to know each other better outside of the office. Alex found it ironic that he had to fly all the way to Japan to get to know his own company's founders better, but he managed to have quite a few interesting conversations with both Brett Curran and Daniel Greteman. He tried to keep the discussions away from work so that they did not think he was trying to suck up to them, and found that it worked very well. Brett was an avid scuba diver and Daniel a mountain climber. They had plenty to talk about.

The dinner was interesting. Alex had no desire to know what it was he was drinking, but it tasted horrible. He knew all about dishonoring your host from Sayuri and drank it. He decided to drink it quickly so that it would be like taking cough medicine as a kid—one quick swig and then he was done. Why prolong the agony? But as soon as he set his cup down a waiter behind him leaned over and refilled it. He drank it quickly again and it was refilled again. By the third cup he decided to give up and just slowly sip it. That seemed to work much better.

On the third day Elissa asked him if he felt uncomfortable being there. Alex was taken aback and did not know why she had even wondered that. She explained that of everyone on the trip, he was the lowest-ranking manager—his team even lower in rank than him. He shrugged it off but did begin looking around a little more closely at the next meeting. Everyone—other than his team and the founders—were Vice Presidents or Senior Vice Presidents of something or other. The people who probably should have been here to represent the Fantasy games was probably Barney and Karen, but even being lower on the organization chart than everyone else Alex did not feel uncomfortable at all. He belonged at this table, doing what he was doing even if his rank did not reflect that.

He was pleased at least to see that nobody—from either company—treated him or his team any differently than anyone else. It was possible some people just assumed he was a Vice President already, but whether they knew or not they all accepted him as an equal.

By Friday, Alex had several archive boxes full of notes, specifications, demos, and proposals for new games on the horizon. Mayumi Aihara, the woman who had served tea at the very first meeting when he arrived, had promised to see that the boxes were all delivered to his office in Worcester for him.

Before flying out early Saturday morning, Sayuri invited Alex to come to dinner with her family. After a week of work, it would be a non-working engagement, but still, with the CEO of Takato Games. Alex asked Elissa to come with him as well, but did not extend the invite to Doug and Everton—after the long week, he got the distinct impression that both were much happier with a night's sleep before the morning flight anyway.

The car arrived at the hotel to pick Alex and Elissa up and then drove them to the private home of Tomiro Takato. Alex was impressed by the grounds and everything he saw. It was like something out of a movie; the estate was built right by the water, with what looked like a bamboo fence around the grounds with vast and breathtaking gardens within.

Alex and Elissa were led to the front entryway—the

Genkan—where they were to take off their shoes, place them into a getabako—a small cabinet that was lower than the entryway—step up onto a raised floor, put on slippers, and then enter the home. The inside was also quite different than anything Alex had ever seen with sliding doors made of wood and paper that served as partitions between rooms, plenty of windows for lighting to be able to flow through the entire house, and mats woven from rice straw atop most of the wooden floors.

Sayuri was the first to greet them and Alex wondered if he had overdressed for the occasion. He had on a suit and Elissa a gown that would be fitting for a formal night out—but Sayuri was in a casual red silk kimono with patterns of cherry blossoms on it.

"Welcome Adams-San, King-San," she said with a bow to each.

"Is it inappropriate for a hug?" Alex asked. It must not have been because Sayuri stepped closer and they embraced.

Koichi stepped into the entryway and bowed as well. Like his sister he was wearing a kimono, though his was beige and had designs of dragons on them. "This way," he instructed.

Alex and Elissa followed the siblings further into the house and found their parents sitting upon the floor by a small table that was set for their meal. Like Sayuri and Koichi they were both wearing kimonos—Tomiro had a navy one similar to Koichi's with dragons on it, whereas his wife Atsuko wore a white kimono with peacocks and cherry blossoms.

Both Tomiro and Atsuko stood up and bowed to welcome their visitors. "Welcome to our home," Tomiro said.

Alex and Elissa both bowed in return. "It is an honor to be invited," Alex replied.

"Come, sit," Tomiro prompted.

Alex and Elissa both sat as the rest of the Takato's did as well. "This is a lovely home you have. The gardens alone are breathtaking," Alex said.

"Why thank you," Atsuko said, looking proud that her efforts were appreciated.

"Sayuri tells me you were one of her classmates at Harvard," Tomiro said.

"We were," Alex confirmed. "We shared several classes together and also were on the same team for a few projects."

"She speaks most fondly of you," Tomiro said. "She feels that your presence in Creative Visions will go a long way to seeing this merger be a success."

"I am honored that she would feel that way," Alex said.

"Your specialty is Fantasy, yes?"

"It is, yes," Alex confirmed. "My team manages and releases the most fantasy games a year for CVE."

"It is important to remember the value of your team," Tomiro said. "One is only as strong as their weakest link. Their success or failure is your own."

"I agree completely," Alex said.

"Alex has a tendency of sharing success by pointing out the contributions of the individuals of the team, but whenever anything goes wrong it all falls on his shoulders. No blame ever goes beyond him," Elissa added.

"An admirable quality," Tomiro said. "Most admirable." He then looked at Sayuri. "I do believe my daughter has good instincts. You are indeed a worthy executive whom we can trust."

"Thank you," Alex said.

"I will be sending Sayuri to the United States in two months time. She will stay there until the merger is complete. She will be the liaison between the current Creative Visions Entertainment and Takato Games. I trust that you two will work together as well with the merger as you had in college."

"I don't have a single doubt in my mind," Alex said.

"Splendid. Then enough business for one night. Let us enjoy our dinner together to celebrate our new union."

Dinner was quite enjoyable, and business did not come up again, but Alex could not stop wondering what doors had suddenly opened for him and his team through this little dinner and turn of events. Would the merger and the fact that he had a connection to the Takato's see him promoted and given even more responsibility and exposure? If it did, he was ready for the opportunities that that would bring. He would embrace it. He actually looked forward to it.

6

Crystal was waiting for Alex when he arrived home. She had been circling around until he emerged—she would have stayed by the terminal exit but a police officer yelled at her and told her to move. She popped the trunk so Alex could put his luggage in and then he slid into the car beside her.

She saw Elissa, Doug, and Everton coming out at the same time and waved to them as they went to their respective rides or cabs.

"I've missed you so much," Alex said after closing the door.

"I've missed you more," she replied.

Crystal turned out of Logan and got back on route 93 where they had to pay a toll for leaving the airport. She followed that to the Mass Pike and then got off at the 128 exit, which she followed to route 9 and then home.

"How was the trip?" Crystal asked.

"Very productive," Alex said. "Thanks to Sayuri I got to meet with her father personally. He said some... interesting things."

"Interesting is good," Crystal said.

"It might be very good," Alex replied, replaying their dinner. "I get the impression that he wants me to have a much bigger hands on approach to this conversion. There might be a promotion in it."

"A promotion would be good," Crystal said.

"I agree," Alex said. "But I don't want to get ahead of myself here. The conversion plan that we discussed is going to take two years. It's a slow merger with things beginning to blend. New ideas will be mutually reviewed and built, but all teams will be integrated, responsibilities divided. It should be interesting."

"Even more late nights for you, no doubt," Crystal said.

Alex looked at her and saw her pouting. "I'm sorry," he said. "I'll try not to get so consumed with my work."

Crystal laughed at that. "I knew when I married you that you were an aggressive go-getter. You wouldn't be the man I fell in love with if you didn't rise to the challenge and grab the bull by the horns."

"Grab the bull by the horns?" Alex asked, looking questioningly at her. "When did you begin using phrases like that?"

"I guess bulls are on my mind," Crystal shrugged. "My

next shoot is on a bull surrounded by cowboys."

"Oh really?"

"Why? You jealous?"

"As long as the cowboys don't get to take you home at night I think we'll be okay," Alex replied. "What's the shoot for?"

"Believe it or not, perfume," Crystal snickered. "The scent that tames even the strongest man."

"Uh oh," Alex replied. "I'll have to be careful in case you try using it on me."

"I don't have to. I've already got you tamed."

"Ouch," Alex said. "You sure know how to keep my ego in check."

"Didn't you read the marriage certificate? I doubly serve as wife and superego."

"I must have missed that part," Alex replied. "But you can make sure I stay in line any day."

"Don't worry, it's a pretty easy job. You're rather predictable."

"Ouch again," Alex said with a laugh.

"I know what motivates you," Crystal replied. "Understanding that helps me to see things through your eyes."

Crystal pulled into their driveway and turned the engine off. Alex got out and walked around the car. As Crystal got out, he pulled her into a hug and then after a minute began kissing her passionately.

In between breaths Crystal looked around. "What will the neighbors think?"

"They'll think I'm a lucky man," Alex said. The luggage momentarily forgotten he swooped her up into his arms and carried her to the door, opened it, and through the threshold. He kicked the door behind him and carried her up to the bedroom. He could see that she had already been prepared. There were roses by the bed, candles waiting to be lit arranged around the room. "You were ready for us."

"No, this was just leftovers from all the lovers I had while you were away."

Alex tossed her into the bed in response and shook his head back and forth mockingly. He then began lighting the candles as she picked up the remote and pushed the button to have the shades close and leave them with only the candlelight.

"Welcome home, Mr. Adams," Crystal said as she pulled the string of her blouse and the top flowed open.

"Why thank you, Mrs. Adams," Alex said as he kneeled on the bed and climbed over to be with her.

She had missed him. She had missed being with him. She was glad he was home. She could feel him on top of her and knew just how much he missed her, too. Crystal began kissing him, enjoying every moment of their reunion. It was good to have him home. Really good.

7

Alex had not responded well to the alarm blaring on Monday morning. He felt like he could sleep for a month and still not be ready to wake up and get into his normal routine. But his sense of responsibility got him out of bed and ready for work. There was a lot to be done following up on everything that was planned out for the merger as well as catching up on what was missed on his existing projects.

As Alex pulled into the parking lot he saw construction vehicles and men with hardhats milling around. He wondered whether they were going to be adding to the existing office to grow it as part of the merger—make more office space for their Japanese colleagues.

Alex walked into the front door and saw Bob Healey, the security guard sitting at the desk. From the very first time he interviewed here he had been pleasant to Bob. Bob was an older man with graying hair and proud of being a new grandfather. The day of his interview the man in front of him had been overly rude and nasty. Alex just made some jokes, laughed, and was pleasant. He and Bob were on a first name basis ever since.

"Morning Bob. What's going on with the construction crew?"

"Changing the pipes," Bob said. "Something to do with a leak that they are trying to fix. Their plans show a gradual digging up of the entire parking lot, changing pipes, and then repaving a section at a time."

"Sounds like fun," Alex replied sarcastically.

"Yeah, real fun. I've been getting complaints because their construction vehicles are slowing down traffic... and this is only the third day they've been here."

"How long is it supposed to take?"

"Not specified, but if you ask me, I wouldn't be surprised in the least if they were still out there a year from now."

"Wonderful," Alex said. "How's Martha and the kids?"

"Can't complain," Bob said. "My daughter is going on a cruise with her husband. We're getting the kids. Should be fun."

"You and Martha going to spoil them rotten?"

"Isn't that in the grandparent's rulebook?" Bob replied.

"Good for you," Alex said. "Have a good one Bob, send

my love to Martha."

"And you to Crystal."

"I will," Alex said.

"Have a good day."

"We'll certainly try," Alex said. He bypassed the elevator and jogged up the stairs to the fifth floor where his office was. He had come in earlier than usual to make sure that he had time to go over any updates and reports from when he was in Japan. He also wanted to schedule a review meeting with his team to see exactly where they were and also to provide some insight into the merger and what was coming their way.

He was surprised to see Karen already there.

"Good morning, Karen. You're here early."

"I figured you would be," she said. "I wanted to talk to you before you got started."

"What's up?" Alex asked.

"Let's talk about your trip first. How did it go?"

"It couldn't have gone better," Alex said. He then spent a few minutes filling her in on the high level points of the week, some of the things he got out of it, and the basic gameplan for the merger.

"I'm going to keep you on the conversion committee," Karen said. "You'll be representing our division."

"I thought I already was," Alex said.

"Well, it's official," Karen replied.

"Good. I felt really comfortable doing it," Alex said.

"I know you'll make me proud," Karen replied. "Which is why I wanted to let you know that I have submitted paperwork to have you promoted."

"Promoted?" Alex asked, grinning. It happened more quickly than he had expected.

"You've earned it," Karen said. "You've more than earned it."

"Thank you," Alex said, keeping things humble.

"It won't happen right away. There's a process and these things take time, but the paperwork has been submitted so it will go through eventually."

"I guess I can be patient for that extra week of vacation," Alex teased.

"And the raise," Karen pointed out.

"Naturally," Alex said.

"There's something else," Karen said. "I don't want you to think I'm upset by your walking into Barney's office last week and asking to be put on the merger. You know I've always respected your aggressive approach and appreciate it."

"But?"

"But I'm not always going to be here," Karen said. "Just keep in mind that not everyone is like me. Some people might be... well, let's just say put off by your approach. Intimidated even."

Alex regarded Karen. Was she going someplace? Why were they having this conversation? And whom had he intimidated? Barney? "Is there a reason we're having this chat? Has someone complained? You know I prefer to face issues personally."

"Sometimes you have to let me do my job," Karen said. "While I'm here."

"Are you thinking of going somewhere?" Alex asked, deciding that getting to the heart of the matter was better than beating around the bush.

"I'm thinking about it," Karen admitted. "Nothing official, so please keep that between us."

"My lips are sealed," Alex said. "Are you looking to go somewhere else?"

"No, not really," Karen said. "I'm thinking... well, I'm thinking about being a stay-at-home mom."

It took Alex a moment before what she said registered. Since he had worked here Karen had had a pair of miscarriages. He knew how much she wanted children and how devastated she was both times she failed to carry the baby to term.

"Karen, are you pregnant?"

He could see tears welling up in her eyes. "I am," she said. "We waited before we told anyone. We didn't want to get our hopes up again. But I'm in my eleventh week. I've never reached my eleventh week before. The doctor seems optimistic that this time I'll make it."

"Karen, congratulations!" Alex said, giving her a hug. "We should have a party to celebrate."

"I'm not letting anyone know until I begin to show," Karen said. "There's a lot to be done between now and then."

Alex could respect that. If Barney caught wind that Karen was pregnant and even considering leaving, he would begin giving more projects to her counterpart—Sandra Murphy—and her team. As long as Karen was here, the bulk of the merger projects would still come to Karen first. Alex had never worked with Sandra, but her reputation preceded her—she was someone who allegedly was very hard to work with or for. Karen on the other hand was just as aggressive as him. He had never seen anyone else work so hard in his life, and like him, she just kept taking more and more on. If she were to leave, it would be a huge blow to CVE and the Fantasy division.

"Well, I'll let you get to work," Karen said.

"Thanks, congratulations again."

"Thank you," Karen said as she returned to her office.

Alex turned his computer on and logged into email. Even using his blackberry in Japan, he still had over three hundred emails waiting for him. He went through all meeting requests first so that his calendar was updated and then looked for a time slot where he could meet with his team. He found time open at 10:00 AM and scheduled it. When he was done he got an invite request from Karen for a debrief meeting at 2:00. He accepted the meeting and glanced at the attendees—it would be Karen, Barney, Sandra, and himself. Looks like he'd be finding out if Sandra's reputation was well deserved or not soon enough.

He then went to the emails, scrolling through for similar themes and staying with one project and then moving on to the other. He began with the quick emails—the company announcements, the random updates, and reminders—to get them out of the way and then went into the projects by priority. As people began arriving for the day he had already managed to get through about half of his emails. By the time he was ready for the 10:00 meeting he was caught up.

Alex tried not to speak much during his team meeting. He asked for updates on where they were and what he missed and let the rest of his team fill him, Elissa, Doug, and Everton in. He did speak briefly about the Tokyo trip, but did not get into any specifics about what was coming down the pipeline, especially with the afternoon meeting with Barney. He was not sure how the work was going to be distributed, so best not to entice his team with something that may never come to pass.

The boxes from Japan arrived around lunchtime and Alex signed for them. He set them down at his desk and began going through them, creating piles of material based on what they were. There was so much useful information in there, but until he knew exactly what was going to be his it only served as background details.

Alex walked into the conference room that Karen reserved and saw Sandra sitting there already. "Hi there," Alex said. "We haven't really done much more than pass each other in the hall. I'm Alex Adams."

Sandra looked at his outstretched hand as if it were infectious and going to contaminate her. He watched as her lip curved into a sneer but she did reach out and shake his hand. "I know who you are."

Well, this is pleasant, Alex thought.

Barney and Karen walked in together and sat down. Alex backstepped and closed the door so that they would have their privacy and then sat down too.

"I asked Karen to schedule this meeting so we all could come together and get on the same page with the migration and integration with Takato Games," Barney said. "Alex had volunteered to go to Japan to represent us and has plenty of information to share."

Alex thought he had done a little more than volunteer to go. He thought he had aggressively gone after the merger and made it his own. He remembered what Karen said about intimidating others with his approach and decided to tread lightly.

"Alex, could you give us an overview of what you learned on the trip?" Barney asked.

"It would be my pleasure," he said. Alex then went into the various meetings with the Takato Games executives and described the process that was agreed upon. Essentially there were a variety of meetings that were being set up on a daily, weekly, and bi-weekly basis to cover different attributes of the integration. The first meeting would be Wednesday internally at CVE with the executives of each area involved in the integration. There also would be a weekly joint-call with Japan every Monday night at 8:00.

"Since Alex has already become familiar with the people managing the conversion, I recommend that he still represent our division in these meetings," Karen said. "Any take-aways that impact us or our teams he could then relay."

That's exactly what Alex wanted. Everything would filter through his fingers first and then be distributed to the appropriate individuals. He hoped that Barney did not object.

Barney looked at Sandra. "Sandra, do you have any objections?"

"If he wants to do it, let him," Sandra said dismissively.

Alex listened to the words but heard something one of his college suitemates had always said: "Better him than me." He wondered how she got to be a vice president with an attitude like that. Perhaps some of the rumors of her reputation were true. The less she had to do with Takato Games the better as far as he was concerned.

"Very well then," Barney said. "Alex, the meetings are all yours. If you have any problems, can't handle the added work load, or see that your current projects are slipping, let Karen know and we'll make other arrangements."

Barney obviously did not know him very well if he was

serious about that. There was no way anything would slip. He would see to it personally. "Of course," Alex said, replying diplomatically.

"This was good. Thank you. I look forward to seeing what other little changes the merger will bring," Barney said. He then stood up, opened the door, and walked out.

Sandra was right behind him without saying a word.

Karen remained in the room with Alex. "You did good."

"Thanks," Alex said.

"I know you, and what Barney said you probably figure you'll never do, right?"

Alex grinned. She knew him so well. They really were cut from the same cloth. "Something like that."

"Well, just remember I'm here if you do need help or support. Don't hesitate to come to me."

"I won't," Alex said, though he doubted he would need to. He basically got the green light that this merger was his—at least for the Fantasy division. There was no way he would let such a high-exposure assignment falter or have any issues. He would meet the challenges, seize the opportunities, and prove that the faith Karen and Tomiro had in him were well deserved.

8

The next few months were a blur. Alex could not remember ever being so busy in his life and he loved every minute of it. The original meetings set up quickly multiplied, almost exponentially, and he spent almost every scheduled moment of the day in meetings or trying to squeeze in work between meetings. But even with the extra work load, not a single deadline was missed and all of his existing projects continued nearly flawlessly.

Sayuri Takato arrived in late March and was set up in a condo near the office. She brought a team of her own with her, including a pair of developers—Yuzo Kanai and Taichi Omata; a quality control tester—Sumio Uwabo; a marketing director—Seiji Yoshida; and Mayumi Aihara to serve as her personal assistant.

Alex and Sayuri worked together to integrate the two

teams into one and focus on the new projects that were coming down the pipeline. Each individual team still had their own work where the opposite tried to observe and learn how the projects were run and designed, but anything new they did together. Both were quite pleased with how quickly the teams began working together.

The integrated team also attracted the attention of Brett and Daniel and were quickly referenced in senior executive meetings as the poster-team for what the integration should mean and how it should be handled. Both Alex and Sayuri were honored by the high praise that they received for their effectiveness of their new team.

Tomiro and his son Koichi visited on several occasions and always tended to focus on the Fantasy team and how Sayuri was adapting to the new assignment. Alex always got the impression from Sayuri's father that he too was quite pleased with their progress. They were highly efficient, ahead of schedule, and taking on more and more responsibility as other teams in the company struggled to meet the demands of the aggressive merger.

Alex wondered from time to time if people who were struggling would wind up losing their jobs in some form of layoff. He suspected that both companies would have some kind of headcount reduction since both had teams of employees doing essentially the same thing. It only made sense. But if there were to be layoffs, he was also confident that it would not impact his team. They had too high of exposure and were too successful to be open to reduction—at least he hoped that was the case.

It was not long before jobs did start to begin to be lost. From the Fantasy division, Sandra Murphy lost half of her staff in a single day. Not a single project manager, or member of any team under Karen Talbott, were touched. Alex was thankful for that fact.

In early July Karen made it official that she was not intending to return from maternity leave. She planned on working right up until she was ready to have the baby, but then she was not coming back. Alex had been prepared, but the announcement sent a ripple of shock through the division with a lot of people wondering what would happen and how that would impact them. Alex decided to be proactive and aggressive and see if he could help ease the transition. His promotion still had not come through, but perhaps with an opening even higher up he could accelerate that and keep the team together without much change.

He walked into Barney's office, knocking on the door as he walked in. Barney glanced up and waved for him to come in. Alex closed the door behind him.

"Something the matter?" Barney asked.

"Just something I wanted to talk to you about," Alex said.

Barney leaned back from his computer and looked at Alex, beckoning him to continue.

"As you know, I have been representing the Fantasy division for some time now in the merger with Takato Games. My team has also been used as an example by both Brett Curran and Daniel Greteman here at CVE, as well as by Tomiro Takato at Takato Games. The exposure my team has created has increased our division's budget and our image within the company."

Alex studied Barney as he spoke, wondering if he was laying it on a bit thick. But he was about to make a bold statement and proposal and he wanted Barney to have the wins in the back of his mind as he did.

"Your team has been very successful, yes," Barney said. "You've also managed this merger flawlessly. The fact that I don't hear issues or complaints is a testament to that."

"Thank you," Alex said, knowing all too well how many other representatives he worked with complained about overbearing egos, uncooperative individuals, and overly demanding deadlines. "The announcement of Karen's departure has hit everyone hard, but I believe I have a solution that will help make a smooth transition."

Barney steepled his fingers together and leaned back in his chair. Not the best body language, but Alex pushed ahead.

"I think that Sayuri could replace me as lead project manager for my team with Elissa largely taking the role Sayuri has now."

"You want Sayuri to take your job?"

"I want someone I trust running the projects, and I trust

Sayuri. I know she will do a good job for me."

"For you?" Barney asked. "I don't understand."

"I would like to be considered for the replacement of Karen," Alex said. "I've already shown that I can run a highly effective team, and now a multi-cultural and integrated team. I also already represent our division, a role that really should have been Karen's and not mine, so technically I am doing her job already. By expanding to include her role I would be gaining two more project managers and teams. I am ready to do so."

Barney exhaled and did not look overly amused. "You already are up for a promotion."

"One has nothing to do with the other," Alex said. "I am the most qualified internal candidate. With my reputation with the ownership of both CVE and Takato Games, I'm sure an exception can be made. I am ready for this role. I will not let you down."

"I'll think about it," Barney promised.

"Thank you, that's all I can ask," Alex said as he got up, opened the door, and left Barney alone. If Barney thought about it or not Alex would never know. He never discussed it with Barney again, and Sandra Murphy was named as successor to Karen. She absorbed all of Karen's project managers into the remnants of her own group and she became the sole individual reporting in to Barney with everyone else below her.

On Karen's last day she and Alex went out to lunch. She

warned him that things were going to change and he had to be ready to change with them. That while she did not mind him walking into Barney's office and trying to get the job she was leaving, Sandra took it as a personal attack against her qualifications. She also told him that she and Sandra had never gotten along and had always had vast differences of opinions and approach to work. Since she and Alex got along so well, that probably would mean Sandra would be threatened by him as she was Karen and their relationship could be strained.

She urged him to give it time, to try and see things from Sandra's perspective, and to do his best not to rock the boat or come across as too heavily handed. Alex promised to try his best, but did not see how he could really change. He was who he was and being that individual had always brought him success. He was not about to change his methods because his new boss was threatened by him.

He had no idea at that lunch just what an ordeal working for Sandra would create, and how it would impact every aspect of his life. If only he knew. But he did not, and there was no way he could have ever predicted what was about to unfold.

9

A week after Karen left and Alex was officially working for Sandra, he did not see much of a change to the way things had been. He and Karen always had a great working relationship. She knew what he could do and he did it. With Sandra that foundation was not there, but largely she was leaving him alone at the moment. He just went to his meetings, facilitated others, and kept driving his projects toward success.

In fact, the only interaction he even had with Sandra at all was the first morning when she stopped by his desk and asked him to send to her the support documentation—initial proposals, analysis documents, concept designs, game specifications, test plans, and any launch materials already prepared—for all of his projects. Alex had it to her within the hour including a document he created with a detailed overview of each project, where they were on it, who were the key resources working on it, and anticipated timelines.

He assumed that she was pleased with the thoroughness and promptness of his materials because he never heard anything to the contrary. As far as he was concerned, a smooth transition would be beneficial. There were a lot of issues in the division where people seemed to sit around and not do a whole lot, or struggled with their projects, or fell behind and consistently missed deadlines, or lost control of the projects completely. Not even one of Alex's projects had ever even come close to some of the things he heard other people talk about. His team was efficient, effective, and consistently busy—just the way he liked it.

One of the other project managers who used to work for Karen, Theresa Zahn, asked Alex if he wanted to do lunch one day. The first time it fit into their schedules was Friday. He, Theresa, and Elissa all went to lunch at the Picadilly Pub. He and Theresa had always gotten along well. She was one of the more competent project managers in the division, and she had over twenty years' experience. She originally worked in finance, and then was lured to Creative Visions when it first opened for the promise of more money, more flexibility with her hours—she was raising a family and found the demands of finance to be a bit stifling—and overall more enjoyable working on games than the latest cutting edge technological enhancement to help clients buy stocks more efficiently than they had before.

They had not done so in a while, but Karen used to have a staff meeting held monthly at various restaurants. She would bring her project managers out and discuss what was going on over a good meal. It was an opportunity to get everyone out of the office and get to know each other better than you would sitting across from them in a conference room. As things got busier with the Takato merger, the ability to go out seemed to lessen considerably. Alex had never been out to lunch with Theresa other than during those meetings. He assumed she wanted to discuss the department's reorg. He only had to wait until their orders were placed for her to begin.

"So what do you think of Sandra?" Theresa asked.

"Not much, to be honest," Alex shrugged. "Karen gave me some tips before she left, but nothing seems to have changed."

Theresa frowned, then glanced at Elissa. "How about you?"

"I haven't even talked to her," Elissa said.

"You two are in for a rude awakening," Theresa scoffed. "This has been a nightmare."

"What do you mean?" Alex asked.

"Did you know I used to work for Sandra before I switched to Karen's team?"

"I did not, no," Alex said.

"Let's just say that Sandra's and my relationship was a

bit... strained," Theresa said. "I would tend to think, just by knowing you, that you'll find the same thing."

"In what way?"

"You think for yourself," Theresa said. "That doesn't go over very well with Sandra."

Alex exchanged a glance with Elissa. What was that supposed to mean? "It's our jobs to think."

"Not in Sandra's world," Theresa scoffed again. "She doesn't tolerate independent thought. Everyone who works for her needs to be sheep that do things exactly as she wants. If anyone shows any initiative or independence, she cuts them down and tries to reign them back in."

"Initiative and independent thought is how we add value to this team," Alex said, not sure he believed Theresa. How could any manager not want their people to work as productively as possible? Especially in the game industry—thinking outside of the box and innovation is what leapt you over your competitors.

"Oh yeah, rude awakening," Theresa said. "I'm surprised you haven't seen it yet. She's already taking control of my projects."

"In what way?"

"She doesn't even let me run my own meetings anymore. She's been coming and facilitating them. The only problem, she doesn't have the slightest clue what the hell she's talking about or doing. She'll take over, then demand people explain things to her again and again and again until she supposedly has it, and then at the end makes me recap everything because she's still clueless."

"Maybe she's just trying to become more familiar with the projects she's inheriting," Elissa speculated.

"This behavior is no different from what she did when I worked for her before," Theresa replied. "She doesn't know anything about games, but somewhere along the way she got her lips permanently puckered onto somebody's ass and managed to get this job and job security. You'll find it maddening how incompetent and inept she is. She'll begin changing things that shouldn't be changed, derail everything you've been doing, and then blame it all on you for not knowing how to do your job properly."

Alex did not like the sound of that at all. Especially when added to Karen's warning before she left. But Sandra had not interfered with him. Shouldn't he give her the benefit of the doubt? Maybe his impression of Theresa was not as accurate as he thought it was. Maybe Sandra recognized Alex's obvious talent and was leaving him alone, but found some kind of deficiency in Theresa and felt the need to take more control.

"That's horrible," Elissa said.

"To say she's a micro-manager is also an understatement," Theresa said, rolling her eyes. "That woman will tear everything you do apart."

"I don't know, I haven't seen it," Alex said.

"That's because she hasn't hit you yet," Theresa

laughed. "But you wait, she will. The fact you have so much more than everyone else is probably why she's hitting you last. The rest of us she was able to begin making her little *improvements* to almost right away."

Alex had to admit that that was at least plausible. He did have far more than anyone else. If Sandra wanted to change the way everyone did business and be far more hands-on than Karen ever was, then it made sense to take on the projects of the managers who only had a handful before tackling his—he had more than all of Karen's other project managers combined.

"I guess I'll deal with it when it comes," Alex said.

"It's more than just her methods," Theresa added. "You especially will have trouble."

"What makes you think that? Because I'm independent?"

"That, but also the fact that you're a man."

"Excuse me?" Alex asked, shocked that his gender had anything to do with anything.

"When we get back to the office, open your eyes and look around. If you see even one man on Sandra's team I'll retract my statement."

Alex thought about it. There was one man on Sandra's team, but he was recently let go. "You're saying she has a problem with men?"

"She is extremely biased and sexist," Theresa said. She then looked at Elissa. "But don't think we're safe just because we're women."

"What do you mean?" Elissa asked.

"We had a 'bring your children to work' day one time. It was company sponsored. There were activities for the parents and children to do, and it was a half-day for those people who participated. I brought my kids. I wanted them to see what I did. Do you know how excited they were when they got to see that their Mommy made video games? It was like I was better than a firefighter," Theresa joked. "But then Sandra did her best to ruin it all. She demanded that the kids leave, that they do the activities without me and I continue to work, and when it was time to leave she told me to call my husband and have them pick the kids up or take a vacation day."

"She can't do that," Alex said. "Company sponsored event."

"Every event is left to managers discretion," Theresa said. "Sandra has no kids. Never had a family. She doesn't understand why I wouldn't want to be at my desk twenty-four hours a day. To even think of the possibility of having kids at work and interrupting the normal flow of the day is unimaginable."

"I can't believe that," Elissa said.

"It's true," Theresa said. "I have the battle scars to prove it. Oh, and don't even think about calling in sick because your kids are sick."

"Of course I'd call in if my kids were sick," Elissa replied. "I'd have to take care of them. Alex understands. I try to work from home as much as I can."

"Trust me," Theresa warned. "If your kids are sick, *you* are sick. If you mention your children at all, whereas most bosses would be understanding and sympathetic, she'll be anything but. I had to bring my son to the hospital one time he was so sick. The doctors were worried that he might not make it. He was burning up. Of course I called in. What parent wouldn't? But Sandra told me that if I was not sick then this did not count as a sick day and I either had to come in immediately, use a vacation day, or she would accept my immediate resignation."

"That's horrible," Elissa said. "I'm a single mom. It's not like I have someone who can watch them if they are sick."

"You'll never have to," Alex said. "You still call in to me and she'll never have to know."

"As long as you know that you'll have to lie to cover for her," Theresa said. "I can't emphasize this enough. Please learn from my experiences."

"Is it only you?" Alex asked, wanting to know if Sandra was really this bad or just had some kind of personal vendetta against Theresa.

"No. There were a bunch of us on the old team. Most left because they couldn't take her. I was fortunate enough to be switched to another team. Obviously we don't have that option now. At least not at the moment."

The waitress returned with their lunch, giving Alex a

moment to think about everything that both Theresa and Karen had said. He had to admit that even before this transition he always got a bad vibe from Sandra. The few times she was in the same room for a meeting or even passing her in the hall she just carried herself with a certain edge that screamed *leave me alone*! Since he had no reason to really interact with her, he had always accepted her body language for what it was and did little more than a slight smirk to signify some form of greeting or pleasantries while passing. She did not even offer that much.

Alex did not like where his thoughts were drifting. He was not one to worry about the *what if's* in the world. He did not beat himself up worrying about what could be, but faced what actually was. Being forewarned was being forearmed as far as he was concerned. He would do his job, be himself, and if Sandra had a problem with that then he would deal with it when the situation arose.

After getting back from lunch Alex looked at his schedule and watch. He had a little time before the week-end status meeting. It was one of the internal status review discussions where each division reported where they were, any pitfalls that they were encountering, and how the integration was progressing. It was one of many meetings he attended on a weekly basis.

He had prepared the materials that he would be asked about before going to lunch and looked them over real quick just to make sure he had not missed something that he wanted to report on. Satisfied that he had everything he picked up his things and headed for the top floor executive conference room, where they would have the session. As he turned to leave his desk he saw Sandra heading for him.

Deciding to be pleasant and not let what Theresa or Karen said impact him, he smiled and said, "Hi Sandra, how are you today?"

She ignored his pleasantries. "You're going to the status call in person?"

"I always do," Alex said. He knew he could call in, but he had always found going to be more beneficial. At his desk he would multitask and did not really pay as close attention because his focus was spit. By going he also got to become more familiar with the higher ups from other areas—it was never a bad idea to network and be visible. His efforts and thoroughness had definitely been helping to augment his already impressive reputation in the company. Besides, when the call ended people often talked, and that was when the true story came out. He learned more in the five minutes following a meeting about how the merger was progressing than he did on the hour-long session.

"That seems to be a waste," Sandra said, frowning.

"I find being at the meetings in person to be quite beneficial," Alex said, wondering if this was the beginning of him having to defend his position and his team.

"I need the dial-in details," Sandra said.

Alex furrowed his brow at that, but quickly recovered. "You'll be joining us today?"

"I want to listen in so that I can determine your role going forward," Sandra said.

My role? Alex did not like the sound of that at all. "Let me just make a copy of the agenda for you."

Sandra followed him to the printer and was impatiently standing over him as he adjusted the setting from print to copy and ran the agenda through. With the agenda she would have all dial-in information, a list of participants, and the speaking points for the meeting.

"Here you go," Alex said.

"See me as soon as the meeting is over," Sandra said and then walked off without another word.

"Okay," Alex said to himself as he exhaled and then walked to his meeting. No matter how much he liked to face things head on, Karen and Theresa's words were flowing through his mind. This was the beginning. He knew it was. Sandra was coming for him and his projects and things were about to change—and change for the worse.

He felt distracted during the meeting, stressed. Other than the things he had to talk about, he could hardly recall much about what was said at all. When the meeting ended he did not even stay for the normal post-meeting discussions. He wanted to confront Sandra and get the inevitable meeting over with.

He walked to her office and knocked. He began to walk in but hesitated, remembering how Karen mentioned that Sandra would have a problem with him knocking on Barney's door and walking in. If she had a problem with that, she might have a problem with him coming into her office, too. So instead he stood at the doorway.

Sandra turned, glared at him, and then back at her computer without saying a word. What did *that* mean?

"Is this a bad time?" Alex asked, thinking about his schedule and everything he had left that he wanted to do before heading home for the weekend. If Sandra heard him, she did not acknowledge it in any way. "Sandra?"

"One minute," she snapped angrily, still looking at her computer and not looking at him.

Alex mock-smiled and waited for her. Waiting was something he was never good at. He was always so busy and always had so much to do that standing around and waiting was a waste of time. Even when working on one thing his mind often swirled with ideas for several other things. He was the classical Type A personality who was overly aggressive, constantly multi-tasking, and did not know how to slow down or stop. In fact, slowing down—even when walking—was so foreign to him that he could not grasp how other people seemed to be able to tolerate working at that pace.

He glanced at his watch. She was making him wait for a

lot longer than a minute. "Let me know when you're ready and I'll come back."

She turned this time, glaring at him again. "I said *one minute!*"

He wanted to counter that she said that five minutes ago, but figured it was not in his best interest to do so. Instead, he bit his lip and waited for her to be ready. He wasted time. Wasted efficiency. He waited, and waited some more. Then she finally turned around and pushed her chair forward to a small round table that was in her office and looked up at him.

"Come in."

Alex stepped into her office and sat down in the chair opposite her. "You wanted to see me?"

"I did, yes," Sandra said. "That meeting you just had, you seem to be on top of it."

"I am," Alex said.

"You don't have any concerns or issues with attending?"

"No," Alex said, deciding to keep it short and to the point so that there would be no confusion.

"I'll let you keep doing it then," Sandra decided. "I certainly don't want to sit through that every day."

Alex did not respond. If she found his meetings boring, then maybe she would leave him alone. But then he decided that something had to be said. He went with a pleasantry for diplomacy. "Thank you."

"It's your other projects that concern me," Sandra said.

"My other projects?" Alex asked, wondering where this was going.

"I've had a chance to look over the materials you gave to me," she said, tapping her finger on a stack of reports. "I want you to go through these and make the changes I have specified."

Changes? Alex reached his hand out, "May I?"

Sandra pushed the pile over to him. "I want these copies back as well as updated drafts of everything."

Alex was confused. Most of the documents were already signed off on and approved. Once that was done a document was locked and you did not reopen it unless there was a major change to the scope of the project. "Most of these are approved already."

"They require new versions," Sandra said. "All of them."

"All of them?" Alex said as he took the top one—an online multi-player role playing game that was one of his prized projects—and flipped through it. The pages were covered with pink ink, crossing out passages, rewording them, and a complete overhaul to what was in print. He could not find a single page without the pink ink practically covering the entire document.

"None of these met my expectations," Sandra said.

Alex studied some of the edits a bit more closely. She appeared to have reworded things in most places. She did not change the requirements or the core of the project, she just did not like the way certain things were worded. He did not see any need to reopen and rewrite the documents and then get them reapproved just because her writing style was different from his.

"Sandra, these edits don't change the project at all. It's a matter of personal preference. I strongly advise against re-opening them and potentially delaying our projects just because you want something worded differently."

As soon as he said it he saw her face turn red as she glared at him. "These documents are unacceptable, and you will rewrite them until I feel that they are. I don't care what you think, or what you advise. I am your manager, not Karen, and you will do things my way. Is that understood?"

Alex knew that this was not going to be a battle he was going to win at the moment. But he also had no intention of slowing down the progress on his projects because he had to rewrite every document that they were working on. He would split things up with Elissa and Junador and not let anyone else know what was going on so that they would not lose two-to-three weeks for differing opinions in sentence structure and formatting.

Alex saw the word Tahoma on every page in big, bold letters and underlined three times. "Tahoma?"

"The font that you will use," Sandra said.

"You're making me switch fonts?"

"It is the font we use," Sandra said.

"It's not a very good font," Alex countered. "It's bulkier,

makes the text longer, and is harder to work with in tables."

"You will use Tahoma 12-point font in every document you produce. Is that understood?" she said, her face turning red again and her eyes gleaming with a look that Alex thought could only be hatred.

He thought changing the font was ridiculous. Who the hell cared about the font used in a document? As long as people could read it and it was functional and professional. But, as she said, she was his manager.

"I'll get my people on it," Alex said.

"No," Sandra said. "You will get on it."

"Excuse me?" Alex asked.

"These are your documents. You do it."

Alex held her gaze for a moment, hardly believing what he was hearing. He wondered if she was trying to set him up to fail. By giving him months of project work to revise, plus trying to keep things progressing as they should, she was basically giving him every opportunity to crash and burn. But she did not know him. He not only would not fail, he would give her exactly what she wanted and far sooner than she even dreamed possible.

"Will that be all?" Alex asked.

Sandra pushed her chair away from the table and turned around back at her computer. Alex sighed. *Guess that was all.*

He gathered the stack of documents and left her office. He walked back to his desk, sat down, saw Elissa looking at him questioningly and mouthed the word "later." He put the stack down, looked at it, and then pushed it aside. He had more important things to do than deal with the crap she wanted done. At least at the moment he did.

Alex finished the rest of his day, but for the first time in a long time left on time. The work would be there for him on Monday morning. By then maybe he would have calmed down from his first meeting with his new boss. Until then, he could not have cared less about Sandra Murphy or her insane demands. Maybe she would be hit by a bus over the weekend and he wouldn't have to be burdened with her busy work. Alex grinned at that thought. If only something like that would actually happen.

10

Theresa turned out to be a prophet. The revision request had only been the beginning. Those, Alex came in bright and early Monday morning with a positive attitude and dove into the pile of requested revisions. He only managed to get through a page before he was rolling his eyes at her requests. Most of them were irrelevant and useless little edits. He could not believe that she was making him take time out of his busy schedule to do such useless and mundane revisions. He had an MIT and Harvard education for goodness sakes—he knew how to write. She just did not like his style.

The fact that these documents had been drafted originally by him, Elissa, or Junador, reviewed by the rest of the team, revised and edited by him, reviewed again, discussed at length, revised yet again to clarify things that needed to be clarified, and then ultimately sent for approval by senior management obviously was lost on her. The amount of effort and consideration put into every document took months to complete, yet Alex had the due diligence to make sure everything was covered, everything was consistent, formatting was superb, and the document was professional. He saw documents that other people had written and could not believe how incomplete and lacking they were. Yet it was his documents that Sandra were ripping apart.

Some of her comments were to remove requirements. She felt that the document was too specific and that Doug and his developers should not be told exactly what to do but have the leeway to come up with the solution on their own. At the same time, Alex recalled numerous meetings with Steven Reed on Doug's team about how he needed more detail on the requirements so that he knew exactly what was expected up front. Sure, he would usually make things better than described, but he needed to know what was being looked for.

Sandra had no idea about his team and the way that they operated. Her changes would handicap them more than help them in a lot of cases. For instances like this, he refused to make the change and added his own red ink in the columns next to her pink writing to explain why he was not making the changes. Another battle, he was sure, but some battles were meant to be fought.

Beyond the revisions, Sandra began attending the meetings that he facilitated. She also told him that she had to be copied on every email he sent, and that if someone from his team did not keep her on the email chain that he had to forward it to her for her review. Everything about her was so different from Karen. With Karen he had completely freedom and autonomy. With Sandra, he was quickly learning that she was trying to make sure he had none.

At the very first meeting she joined him on; he had yet another run in with her. But that was only the beginning. The normal protocol for his meetings was to arrive at the conference room where the meeting was to be held and dial in to the call in case anyone called in instead of coming in person. Elissa always attended with him unless he was double booked and needed her to facilitate another meeting. He would run the meeting and Elissa would take notes. He took notes too, but that was more for his own records and review. It helped to be able to go over them when Elissa gave him a draft of the minutes. When she first began, she always spoke about how she was amazed at his attention to detail for the important speaking points. Things she missed he caught right away. Between them it was a very effective system.

At this meeting, they were discussing a single-player game with a princess who had her kingdom overrun and had to fight back with a combination of storyline elements, amazing graphics, searching for items and equipment, and hack-and-slash functionality—Alex took the role call and then went to begin the meeting but was cut off. Sandra just began speaking over him.

Alex was confused. This was his meeting, but she began running it. His shock was mirrored on the faces of those in the room. Most notably Elissa, Sayuri, Doug Malone, and Everton Taylor. With his role of facilitator apparently taken away, Alex became a participant, but quickly found that his role was really that of clarifier and defender of his team. Sandra kept asking questions that they had discussed months ago and Alex tried to explain it to her and bring her up to speed. His team did not need to waste their time like this, but she would not drop it, demanding to know, not just getting the answers and up to speed, but reopening the discussions and trying to change things to her perspective.

Those shocked looks turned to alarm before the meeting was over. If Sandra had her way, the entire pitch of a "princess" was about to be scrapped and a more-likely heroine was to be born as a soldier who had not been in the kingdom when it was overrun. The game had been in development for months. A fundamental change like that would mean starting completely from scratch for the most part. Nobody was pleased other than Sandra, who walked out of the room when the meeting was done without a parting word.

"Alex, we need to talk," Doug said.

Alex knew what Doug would want to talk about. His

team was the one that was developing the game. Changes like this just weren't acceptable in the gaming community. Not this late in the game.

"He's right, lad," Everton said. "You need to regain control of your team. There's no other way this will work."

"I can talk to my father if you think it would help," Sayuri added.

Alex thought about Karen's warning again. No. Going to Tomiro Takato would make things worse, not better. He would have to fight this battle himself. "Keep things going as is. No changes to the project that was approved. I'll find a way to get her to see that."

"You better," Doug said. "We don't have the budget to waste all the resources we used on this game."

"I hear you," Alex said.

"Maybe you can talk to Barney," Elissa suggested.

"Not yet," Alex said. "I still have to try to find some way to get Sandra and I on the same page. I want to try that first."

"See that you do," Everton said. "This little team of ours is under a microscope. The executives all love us, and other groups all want to see us fail. Remember that."

Alex did not need to be reminded. He was the one who aggressively got his team into the spotlight with this merger. He knew that there were other project managers who resented hearing all about the dream team and how great they were. If Sandra found a way to knock them down a few pegs, it would have ripples throughout the organization.

Alex looked at Elissa. "Can you get me a draft of the Minutes within the hour?" He always liked to have his Minutes—the recap of meetings with all follow-ups captured—go out the same day if possible. Elissa knew that and often got him the draft as quickly as she could. An hour though might be pushing it, but he wanted them done and out before his chat with Sandra.

"I'll do my best," Elissa said.

"You can leave out all of the stuff rehashing what was already agreed upon. You can leave in Sandra's preference for the soldier, but list it as 'Sandra proposed a revision to the agreed upon concept idea' so that it's captured but shown that we're not doing it."

"You sure you want to go that route?" Elissa asked, looking worried.

"I need it in print so that when someone higher up is brought in they'll see just how she is trying to interfere and change things," Alex said.

"You got it," Elissa said. "Just so long as you know that Sandra is not going to be happy."

"I'm beginning to come to expect that," Alex shrugged.

He actually wondered if there was anything in life that did make the woman happy. He had heard her laughing from time to time. Deep belly-laughs that he felt dripped with insincerity. In another chat with Theresa she mentioned how Sandra does a great job if her job description was "kissing Barney's ass." He began paying more attention and saw Sandra going into Barney's office daily, and those loud belly-laughs always seemed to come through the closed door. The more he heard it the more it began sending shivers down his spine.

Elissa managed to have the draft of Minutes down within the hour. Alex looked them over, made a few minor changes, handed them back to her and told her she could send them out as soon as she was done. Five minutes later he saw the email with the Minutes attached. Twenty seconds after that he got an instant message from Sandra asking him to see her.

Alex took a folder with paper in it—for some reason he preferred writing on white printer paper rather than notebook paper—and headed for her office.

Elissa watched him go. "That was fast."

"Too fast," Alex agreed. He walked to her office and knocked. At least this time she did not make him wait. She spun around, her face red and flustered.

"Why did the Minutes go out?" she demanded.

"Excuse me?" Alex asked, not sure what she was getting at. Minutes always went out after a meeting.

"Did I stutter? Why did the Minutes go out?" she repeated.

"Minutes always go out after a meeting," Alex said. "That's standard protocol."

"You didn't show them to me," she said.

"I approve Minutes and send them out," Alex said.

"Unacceptable," Sandra said. "You will recall these Minutes and send out a new draft that has my edits upon them."

Alex bit his tongue. How could she be serious? "There are more pressing business concerns than revising Minutes. Elissa already wrote them, I sent her my revisions, she made the changes, I approved it, and she sent it out."

"You don't have the authority to approve Minutes," Sandra said.

"Excuse me?" Alex scoffed, taken aback. Sending out Minutes was the most mundane and administrative aspect of their jobs. If she didn't even trust him to do that, then what exactly was his role following the transition?

"You heard me," Sandra sneered. "No Minutes will be sent out without my personal review and approval. What you *approved* was inaccurate and incomplete."

Alex knew she was referring to her excessive questions that wasted time. It couldn't possibly be anything else. Karen always expected Minutes to be almost like a ledger of everything discussed. It took him awhile before he was able to capture and provide that much detail. He normally zeroed in on the key points, but even discussions were captured so that several months down the road if there was a problem there was a log of what led to the decision. He trained Elissa the same way. Their Minutes were nothing if not detailed.

"And another thing," Sandra continued. "Why did Elissa write the Minutes?"

Alex felt taken aback again. That was just the structure. Elissa worked for him. He facilitated, she drafted. He even took a course one time on Project Management and the professor had been adamant that the person who runs a meeting should always assign someone else to take the notes. That way the facilitator is focused on the meeting and doesn't miss details or slow things down. A recorder would be responsible for recapping what was discussed. Was Sandra questioning that? A fundamental aspect of being a project manager?

"That's part of her job," Alex replied, knowing that his words had some attitude laced in them. He couldn't keep the attitude out. He usually spoke with people with mutual respect and enthusiasm. But with Sandra, he was quickly beginning to realize that he could not stand the woman.

"Correction, that is your job," Sandra said.

"Actually, Minutes is the job of the recorder, not the facilitator," Alex said.

"You will write your own Minutes from now on," Sandra demanded. "Anyone who runs a meeting will write their own Minutes. There is absolutely no need to waste people's time by having someone else there just to take notes."

Like you wasted time asking useless questions?

"Do you understand me?" Sandra asked.

"There are proven theories on the proper protocol for

running a meeting," Alex said, trying to pull on his knowledge from his instructors.

"Don't you get snide with me," Sandra sneered. "You will write your own Minutes. You will give them to me for approval. I will send them out when I deem that they are good enough to do so. Do you understand me?"

"Fine," Alex said. Maybe he would have to go over her head. This wasn't working.

"Recall the Minutes. I will give you revisions."

"Fine," Alex said again. "Are we through?"

Sandra pivoted her chair around and faced her computer, silently dismissing him. Alex went back to his desk and asked Elissa to send out a follow-up email telling everyone that a revised version of the Minutes would soon be coming out. The word "soon" was apparently an overstatement—Sandra did not submit her change requests for three days. So much for sending out Minutes promptly. Alex made the requested revisions, seeing that there was now references of agreement to adjust the scope and design of the game to switch the princess to a soldier, and sent it back to her so she could send it out like she wanted to. At least when the executives exploded over the wasted time, productivity, and money it will have come from her. He made sure he saved a copy of the original draft of Minutes in case he needed it down the road to use against her. Inevitably, he felt that sooner or later it would be a battle of him against her, and he needed all the ammunition he could find.

11

Crystal sat at the dining room table tapping her fingers. Alex had called three hours ago to let her know he was running late and was going to miss dinner, but she had hoped that he would still be home before this. She knew how stressed he had been since Karen left Creative Visions and wanted to try to give him an evening of romance and relaxation to help him. She had the table set with candles, a small basket of roses for a centerpiece, and she even broke out the fine china and crystal.

For dinner she had got them both Baked Stuffed Lobsters from one of the more upscale restaurants that they enjoyed treating themselves to from time to time. She even had a new chemise for him, along with rose petals scattered across the bed. The sound system was pumping in an orchestra playing romantic music to every room in the house. It would have been perfect if he hadn't gotten stuck at work late again.

She could see how unhappy he was becoming and it worried her tremendously. She knew that most people probably hated their jobs and did it as a means to an end. But they had always been good at their jobs, passionate about them, and driven. It was like seeing a completely different person from before Sandra took over the team to now.

The Alex from before woke up every morning with a smile and a jump to his step. He was anxious to get started, to face the challenges that the day had, and with the confidence and conviction to not only do his job but to exceed all expectations. The Alex now kept resetting his alarm clock and hitting the snooze button, hated getting out of bed, dragged himself like a zombie wherever he was going, and looked like a smile would somehow shatter his face. In a word, he was miserable.

She hated seeing him like this. She wished that he would just walk away from it all, but she knew that Alexander Adams had never walked away from anything a day in his life. But this was one time she felt that he really should consider it. Life was too short to be this distraught all the time. Even if he took some time off, they still had more than enough money to keep them going. Her salary alone was more than most families even hoped to have. But of course, as a model, how many more years would she have before magazines wanted a younger, fresher face. She hated that thought, but it was in the back of her mind. Business was nothing if not cutthroat.

Crystal heard the car pull into the driveway and she got up to meet Alex at the door. This was his night. He needed her now more than ever. She was not going to pressure him, or push him to make a change. She would be there, love him, and let him know that whatever he did she would be there to support him.

He opened the door and she could see that he looked horrible. His eyes were drooped, lifeless. His shoulders were sagging. The top button of his collar was unbuttoned and his tie was pulled down and loosened. He had always taken such pride in his appearance. She was shocked to see him like this.

"Let me help you with that," she said as he was taking his suit jacket off.

"Thanks," he replied, looking like he was about to collapse. "Sorry I'm so late."

"It's okay," Crystal replied. "I can reheat dinner for us."

Alex walked further into the house and froze at the entry to the dining room. He studied the slightly burnt candles, the flowers, and the arrangements. "You had plans tonight? I'm so sorry."

"Don't worry about it," Crystal said. "Sit down. I'll get dinner."

He looked like he was going to protest, but then walked in and sat down in his seat. Crystal smiled affectionately, trying to be encouraging, and then walked into the kitchen to reheat the lobsters in the microwave. She knew that they would never be as good this way, but it was the best she could do.

She was worried about him though. Confrontations and being unhappy at work was one thing. Looking like this was something entirely different. Maybe she should speak up rather than just be here for him.

When the lobsters were done she brought them in and set one down before him and another for herself. He had already poured the wine that had been in the ice bucket, chilling, on the table.

"Wow, this looks fantastic," Alex said.

"I wanted to do something nice for you," she said. "You've been so stressed lately. I thought a night off would be good."

"Thank you," Alex said, the signs of a smile tugging at his lips. It was a start.

"Do you want to talk about it?" Crystal asked, ready to listen or change the topic depending upon his answer.

"I guess," Alex said. "I got a visit today from Sabrina

Stanley and Seiji Yoshida. Do you remember Sabrina?"

"She's the Marketing Director, right?"

"Right. Seiji is her counterpart from Sayuri's team. He got a little, well, to be frank, he got some inside information today. One of our competitors is releasing an online fantasy roleplaying game very similar to ours."

"That doesn't sound unusual," Crystal replied.

"Yeah, but he also heard that the competitor allows users to play multiple characters."

"How does that compare to yours?"

"Ours allows you to build and develop multiple characters, but you can only play with one at a time," Alex explained. "From what Seiji said, the competitor allows you to play with any of your created characters, but the rest still travel and level up with you. The system itself controls them when you are not, but you can jump from one character to another so you can be playing as whoever you want whenever you want."

"Makes sense," Crystal says.

"Yeah, it does," Alex said. "It's a feature that will put our competitor ahead of us. No matter how good ours is, that option will gain more appeal. It's a disaster."

"So what are you going to do?"

"Build that feature into our game," Alex said. "It'll delay the launch by about a year. Maybe a little more. But without that feature we're sunk."

"So you were in meetings discussing that?"

"Yeah," Alex said. "That and other things."

"What aren't you telling me?" Crystal asked.

Alex put his fork down, stared at his dinner, and then looked up at her. "Sandra got up on her soap box and pointed the finger and blame right at me. The added millions to include this feature is my fault. The fact that this wasn't thought of sooner was my fault. The fact that the launch will be delayed is my fault. It's all my fault."

"How could you have known what a competitor would do?" asked Crystal.

"That was my point. But Sandra said that my analysis of the market, the demand, and desired features were flawed, incomplete, and inadequate."

"She said that?"

"She said that," Alex confirmed. "The documentation was perfect. This game has been my baby. I put my heart and soul into it because it's the biggest launch of all of my projects. The most important release. The game that is going to put the joint effort of Creative Visions Entertainment and Takato Games on the map. There was nothing wrong with the documentation. There will be nothing wrong with the documentation once the revisions are signed off on tomorrow. But she would not listen to reason. She just kept lashing out at me, attacking me, pushing me."

Alex paused, then looked back down at his lobster again. "I don't know how much more I can take."

Crystal heard the emotion in his voice and saw a tear flow down his cheek and onto his plate. Seeing him like this killed her. She got up and rushed to him, embracing him and holding him tight. "Whatever happens don't let her beat you."

"Everything I do, everything I try, she just finds fault in it. I do more than anyone and thinks everything is just flawed."

She hesitated before saying it, but did pose the suggestion. "Maybe you should think about leaving."

"I can't expose my team to her," Alex said. "It's bad enough I'm going through this, but at least I'm shielding them."

"Sometimes you need to think about yourself, your needs, what's best for you before you do others."

"I can't abandon them," Alex said. "I just can't."

"Then go to Barney. Tell him what is going on. See if he can help."

"You know, she's in his office every day kissing his ass," Alex said. "I don't know if Barney will be behind me on this one."

"Then go above him. Go to Brett or Dan, or even Sayuri's father. You know all of them now."

"I'd feel like I was in elementary school squealing on the

bully."

"You need to protect yourself," Crystal said.

"I'm documenting everything," Alex sighed. "Keeping a record just in case."

"You might need to do more than that."

"Maybe I'll talk to Barney when I get home from San Francisco," Alex said.

"You mean Sandra hasn't forbidden you from going?" Crystal said, trying to get him to laugh.

"I think she wants me away for a week so she can make some changes behind my back."

"While you're looking out for everyone else, just make sure you're watching your own back, too, okay?"

"I promise," Alex said.

Crystal stood up and began massaging his shoulders. "You're so tense."

"That's an understatement," Alex said, exhaling. "That feels good."

"People will see through her you know," Crystal said. "You and your team don't go from being the poster-team of the company to bottom dwellers overnight for nothing. They know who you are, what you represent, and what you're capable of."

"I know," Alex said. "Most days, anyway."

"Don't you forget it," she said as she leaned over and kissed the back of his head. "But if you ever decide to tell her to just go fuck herself, that's okay, too."

"Oh yeah?" Alex asked.

"Absolutely," Crystal said. "As long as we're together we can overcome anything. We're not defined by our jobs, but by who we are and who we want to be."

Alex closed his eyes, then opened them and tilted his head back to see her. "Thank you. For everything."

Crystal leaned over and kissed him on the lips. The night didn't turn out so bad after all. He let it out, was already looking better, and as she led him upstairs, she knew that it would not be long before he didn't even remember why he was in a bad mood to begin with. This was the way it was supposed to be. In good time and bad, together forever, helping to see each other through the rough spots and cherishing the pleasant times.

12

Alex always looked forward to the annual gaming convention in San Francisco. It was a great way to see what was close to being released and to get excited about potential new ideas and new features that were worth exploring. The overall excitement and enthusiasm of being in the same place as so many gaming professionals was infectious. It was the one time of year people were not competitors but all like kids looking at the new shiny toy and admiring each other's work. He felt fortunate that he had been pre-registered before Karen left—somehow he doubted Sandra would be as willing to sign off on his attending the convention.

He knew his team was more than capable of running things in his absence, but with both he and Sayuri going on the trip and Sandra on her rampage he wanted to make sure there were no issues before going. He decided to make the trip to work to do a few last-minute things, organize a few things, and delegate his duties to people. He also prayed that he did not run into Sandra. She usually did not show up until after 9:00, so he doubted that they would even see each other.

Alex always liked the early mornings at the office. It was quiet and he could get far more done before 8:00 than he could as soon as the first few members of his team began showing up and the flow of the day kicked into overdrive. In the early morning hours he could catch up on his emails, think about his documents, get some writing in, and even help out Elissa and Junador a bit by scheduling meetings, writing Agendas, and sending materials out.

Satisfied that everything he wanted to do before leaving was done, Alex logged off of his computer and got up to leave. As he stood up, Sandra was standing behind him. Alex's eyes widened, the only hint of his shock. "Good morning Sandra," he said to try and be pleasant.

"Have you prepared questions for the 4:00 meeting?" she asked.

"Elissa is going to facilitate the meeting for me while I'm away," Alex said. "She knows what needs to be asked and will be prepared."

Sandra's face grew red, her eyes narrowing. "I will facilitate the meeting! Have questions prepared for me and have Elissa bring them."

"Sure," Alex said, hoping that Sandra would just leave. He had already stayed longer than he should. His luck he would miss his flight and then be stuck here with her for the entire week.

Sandra seemed satisfied that he was going to comply and stormed off back to her own office.

Alex sat back down, turned his computer back on and looked at the clock and his time. Nothing like being in a rush to Logan during rush-hour traffic. He accessed his email and drafted a quick note to Elissa, letting her know that Sandra intended to facilitate the 4:00 meeting but wanted questions prepared to ask at it. He then typed out a dozen questions that were pertinent and should be asked during the meeting. He then wished her luck and clicked send. After the email was out he logged off of his computer again and walked the long way out of the office so that he did not have to go anywhere near Sandra's office.

As he walked out of the office he saw Bob Healey sitting at the security desk. "Have a good week, Bob," he said.

"You heading out already?" Bob asked.

"I'm going to the convention in San Francisco."

"Ooh, that sounds like fun," Bob said.

"Your grandkid is too young to want some free samples, right?"

"Still in diapers," Bob laughed. "But that would have been very thoughtful."

"Maybe next time," Alex said, hoping that there would

be a next time with Sandra as his boss.

"Don't forget to have some fun while you're there too," Bob said. "You work too much. You should enjoy life a bit more."

"My wife would probably agree with you," Alex sighed.

"Have a good trip," Bob added with a wink.

"I'll do my best," Alex promised.

Alex got into his car and headed for the Mass Pike to take him into Logan. As he suspected traffic was horrible. Every time he switched lanes because one looked like it was driving faster than the other it suddenly stopped and he watched with horror as the lane he was in began driving again. Finally he decided to just be patient, stayed in the left lane, and drove.

The toll booths were backed up for what seemed like forever. He wondered why they did not have more people working the booths. For all the glory of the express lanes, he still was stuck there for forty minutes—of course he did not have an express lane device, but he rarely drove on the Pike so why should he?

When he finally arrived at Logan, twenty minutes before his flight was scheduled to take off, he found a very anxious Sayuri pacing as she waited for him.

"Cutting it a little close, aren't you?" she said as she shook her head—but he could see that she was teasing him by how relieved she looked.

"Sorry, I went into the office to get a few things done,"

Alex said.

"Always trying to squeeze one last thing in," Sayuri said. "That's either admirable or foolish."

"Probably both," Alex admitted.

"Probably," Sayuri said with a smirk. "So what was so important that you had to be this late?"

"Well, I would have left earlier than I did, but had another run in with Sandra."

"What did she want now?"

"Questions for the 4:00 meeting. She was furious that I suggested Elissa would run the meeting. She then demanded questions to ask. She should just let Elissa do her job. The meeting would be far more productive with someone who knew what they were doing."

"I could speak to my father if you wish," Sayuri said. "I see the way she treats you. It is undeserved."

"No. Thank you, but no. This is my battle to fight and win," Alex sighed. "These are the times that try men's souls and all that."

"Oh, so working for Sandra is like fighting a war."

"Every day I think fighting in a war might actually be easier," Alex said. "At least there you get to shoot at your enemies."

"Things won't always be like this Alex-san," Sayuri said.

"From your lips to God's ears," Alex said. "So where do I need to go to check in?"

"I already took care of it. We just have to go board."

"They let you do that?"

"I have my ways," Sayuri said with a grin.

He bet she did, but was still surprised that she could do that with all of the heightened security following the 9/11 disaster. But she had been right. They passed right through security, to the boarding gate, and right onto the plane. He felt so relieved when they were in their seats and were able to lean back and relax. The reality of being away from Sandra for a whole week flowed over him. Perhaps he would take Bob's advice and try to have a little fun on this trip, too. The convention was already like a vacation. He was still working, but nothing like his normal day job. But there was no reason not to work for a few hours and then spend the rest of the day for himself.

As against his nature as it would be, he decided that the office could take care of itself this week. He logged into his email from his blackberry and activated an "out of office" message indicating that people should contact Sandra with any questions that they had. He'd rather send them to Elissa, but if Sandra wanted to be in charge, let her see how much he really did on a weekly basis. He hoped she drowned in the waters he safely navigated every single day of his life. The thought of her drowning was the first thing to legitimately put a smile on his face all day. It was enough to keep him happy during take off and most of the flight. Such a beautiful image to think of the suffering Sandra would have gasping for air as water flowed into her lungs.

13

The flight landed in San Francisco in the early afternoon
and Alex and Sayuri took a taxi to the hotel where they
would be staying. They got their rooms, settled in, fresh-
ened up a bit, and then met to go to the convention. It
looked like the gaming convention was even larger this year
than the last. There were lines at registration that went outside and around the corner. Both stood there waiting to get
their badges for almost two hours before they got inside.

Once in it was like a gamers paradise. There were exhibits, demonstrations, competitions, people dressed up as
characters from the games, and information aplenty about
the newest product releases. There also were panel discussions, seminars, and state of the industry debriefs. Alex had
a few of the lectures he wanted to attend, but otherwise

planned on spending the bulk of his time exploring the newest releases and innovations.

Creative Visions and Takato Games both had exhibits. People from marketing and sales manned the booths to discuss the latest releases and what was in the pipeline. Alex and Sayuri both planned on checking in and seeing how things were going at some point during the week.

For about an hour while they were on the main exhibit hall Alex felt like himself again. All thoughts of the home office and Sandra Murphy were gone. It was as if the past few months with her taking over his team had never happened. He enjoyed feeling like himself again. He wished Crystal could see him like this.

Thinking about Crystal he realized how difficult it must be for her ever since Sandra took over. He had been a shell of his former self. Even working the long hours he would still come home every night energetic, excited, and ready to share the experiences from both of their days before. Under Sandra he would come home solemn, tired, and wanting to just be left alone most of the time.

Alex tapped Sayuri on the shoulder. "I want to call Crystal."

"I'll stay with you," Sayuri said.

"You don't have to. Keep looking around."

"We have the whole week. I don't want to risk getting separated and lost."

"Fair enough," Alex said. They left the main exhibit hall and found some presentation rooms that were not currently occupied. Alex held the door open for Sayuri and let her walk in before him.

He pulled out his phone and clicked the speed dial button for Crystal. It was later on the East Coast and he figured she was probably at home eating right about now. As he went to push the send button, the phone rang. He looked at the display and saw that it was Elissa.

"Do great minds think alike?" Sayuri asked.

"No, it's Elissa," Alex said.

"Aren't you going to answer?"

Alex stared at the ringing phone. If he answered the reality of work and Sandra would come crashing back in. He enjoyed being away from her and the problems. But he was never one to ignore his issues. "Yeah, yeah I am."

He then pushed the button to answer the phone and said, "Alexander Adams."

"Sandra sure is pissed at you," Elissa said.

Alex felt an uncontrollable rage come over him. He finally had pushed Sandra behind him and then here she was reaching through the phone line to strangle and stifle him. Without even thinking, he lashed out, letting his anger get the best of him. "Tell Sandra she can go fuck herself! I quit!"

Sayuri's eyes widened as she stared at Alex, silently

mouthing the question "What's wrong?"

Alex felt like taking his phone and throwing it as hard as he could and letting it shatter into a hundred little pieces. He was done with Sandra Murphy. She had pushed him too far.

"Woah, woah, woah, calm down," Elissa said.

Alex just breathed heavily, waging the internal debate of throwing his phone. Deep down he rationalized that if he did he would lose all of his contact information and need to reprogram the phone after getting a new one. There would be a hassle, an irritation, and an inconvenience. That alone kept him from doing what he so desperately wanted to do.

Sayuri walked closer, she put her hands on his shoulder, squeezing to let him know that whatever was wrong he was not alone. Alex could see the compassion and understanding in her eyes. She would understand. She knew him and saw the way Sandra was treating him.

"Alex?" Elissa asked. "Are you still there?"

"I'm here," Alex said, tense, his words bitter. "What is the bitch upset about now?"

"You know those questions you emailed me this morning?"

"Yeah, what about them?" Alex asked, thinking of the dozen questions for Sandra to ask in the 4:00 meeting.

"Well, and please don't get upset again, but Sandra said that you were unprepared, unprofessional, and that the materials you provided were unacceptable."

She could warn him not to get upset all she wanted. He was furious. Sandra asked for questions. He gave her questions. They were the same questions he would have asked to get to the heart of the matter. There was nothing wrong with his questions.

"I sent you what she asked me for," Alex said, unable to keep the anger from his voice.

"Well, apparently questions weren't what she was looking for," Elissa said.

"She asked me for questions, I gave her questions," Alex said. "I almost missed my fucking flight getting her those damned questions. What more did she want?"

"An agenda, action items, follow-up questions, and an issues list."

"Excuse me?" Alex said. "She never asked for any of those things. I don't even use the issues list. I track issues in the follow-ups of Minutes."

"But that's what she expected. Not the questions you provided."

"If that's what she wanted, then that's what she should have fucking asked me for!" Alex shouted.

"You're preaching to the choir here, boss," Elissa said. "I covered for you, said that it must have just been a misunderstanding. That didn't stop Sandra from spending a few minutes in the meeting apologizing for being unprepared and laying the blame all on you."

"Of course she did," Alex said.

"So you're not really quitting, are you?" Elissa asked.

"I'm thinking about it," Alex said.

"That would be bad. Don't let her beat you."

"I'll think about it," Alex said. "Do me a favor. Don't call again. I want this week away to try and clear my head. I trust you to run things while I'm away. Just try not to incur the wrath of our new esteemed leader."

"You forget, she loves me," Elissa said. "I've got the right body parts."

"Ha, ha, very funny," Alex said. "Have a good week."

"Yeah, you too."

Alex hung up and thought again about throwing the phone. Sandra Murphy could get to him more than anyone he had ever known. There was not a single thing about her that was redeeming in the least. She had no interpersonal skills, did not understand the business they were in, ripped people apart, stifled creativity and growth, kissed ass to get ahead, and cared less about her deteriorating appearance than someone who lived on the streets. Everything about her just got under his skin.

Sayuri was still massaging his shoulders. "You're so tense, Alex-san. You need to calm down."

"I know, I'm sorry you had to see that," Alex said. "My outburst was very unprofessional and not very gentlemanly of me."

"We may work together, but I have been your friend longer," she said. "You have no need to apologize or hide your true feelings from me."

"Thank you," Alex said as he reached up and put his hand on hers, squeezing it. "That means a lot to me. Really."

"I think we need to get you to expend some energy," Sayuri said.

Alex turned and looked up at her. "What did you have in mind?"

"The hotel has a gym. I think we should workout. It'll help you clear your mind."

Alex considered it and nodded. A workout would be nice. With every moment he pushed himself to his limits it would be a step closer to clearing his mind of Sandra. If he had his way, he would never have to think about her or be faced with her again. Unfortunately life was not so kind.

14

The rest of the San Francisco trip just was not as good as Alex had hoped it would be. No matter how hard Sayuri tried, he definitely found himself in a funk and was distracted. He tried his best not to ruin it for her, but he just wasn't himself. There was an inevitable confrontation at work and he had to get it over with. Until he did he could not relax and enjoy himself.

Sayuri seemed to understand and sympathize, but Alex could also see the pain in her eyes at seeing him like this. He knew she wished that there was something she could do to make it all better for him. Maybe after the confrontation he would let her. How hard would it be to ask her father to move him to a different department for a while?

Alex was so anxious to get home that they changed their flights and left early Friday morning rather than remaining at the convention and attending the masquerade ball and closing ceremonies Friday night. Sayuri was disappointed, but she did not complain even once.

After reaching Logan Alex and Sayuri parted ways. She wished him luck and he headed to the parking lot and his car to head back to the office. He wasn't sure what he intended to do. He felt like things could go either way. He knew he intended to confront Sandra, but would he defend his position and fight, accept her criticism, or lash back and tender his resignation. Of the three, acceptance was the least likely.

The entire trip to Worcester and work, he prepared his argument in his mind. He tried to visualize just what Sandra would do and say and then prepared a counter argument for everything he imagined. He was as ready as he was going to be, and if this was his last day as an employee of Creative Visions, he could accept that. Crystal was right. It was better to find something else than to sit here and have this woman slowly destroy his life.

Alex waved to Bob as he walked in, ignoring the security guard's question about how the trip was. He did not want to mellow and calm down. He was ready for his confrontation. Sandra is the one he was going to speak with first.

He jogged up the stairs, two at a time, and got off on his floor. He headed right to Sandra's desk and saw that she was not there. He frowned and then began heading to his. He saw her standing by Barney's office. She looked at him, her eyes narrowed, and then she beckoned him with her index finger.

Alex made his way over to her as she turned her back on him and continued speaking with Barney. He stopped next to her. "You wanted to see me?" he asked, deciding to make it seem like this little meeting was all her idea.

Sandra brushed past him, hitting his shoulder as she went and walked into a conference room. Alex could feel the anger bubbling under the surface. Definitely not acceptance.

Barney stood up and walked over. "Alex, how was the trip?"

"Can't complain," Alex said.

"Come on, we'll have a quick chat about it," Barney said as he extended his hand for Alex to go into the conference room Sandra just walked in to.

Alex walked in and Barney followed, closing the door behind him. He then sat down between Alex and Sandra who were on complete opposite ends of the table.

"Alex, I'm glad you came in today. It seems that there has been some tension between you and Sandra and I thought we could air it all out and move forward."

Alex stared, dumbfounded, at Barney. Had Sandra escalated things to Barney before he could? All of this time he did not want to rock the boat any more than he had to and get her even more riled up, but here Barney was and suddenly it was Alex on the defensive.

"Alex, would you like to begin?" Barney asked.

Alex considered it for a moment and then decided that he would let it all out. If Barney fired him or he resigned, then so be it. He was not leaving this room until Barney knew what was going on.

"You know that I run one of the most successful project teams in Creative Strategists," Alex began. "My team has been prominently mentioned by executives of our company and Takato Games as an example for others to aspire to. Yet ever since Sandra has taken over for Karen she has done nothing but work to tear the team apart and destroy everything that we have built."

Barney held his index finger up. "Now, now Alex. We're not here to make things worse by getting nasty. We're here to find a meeting of the minds and move forward."

"Unlikely," Alex snorted. "I have tried since Sandra took over to get her what she wants. But no matter how hard I try or what I do she finds fault with everything and seems hell bent on seeing me fail."

"I believe that is a bit harsh," Barney said. "Obviously the goal here is for you to succeed. We're all looking for success. Sandra merely is trying to help you grow and achieve even greater success."

"By holding me back? By micro managing every single little thing? Did you know she made me open up documents that were already signed-off on just because she wanted sentences written a little differently? That's insane!"

"Sandra has a very different management style than Karen, agreed," Barney said. "But just because hers is different does not mean its wrong. It's your confrontational attitude and inflexibility to change that is causing problems here."

Alex bit his lip. Sandra had already gotten to Barney. All of her ass kissing was now paying off. Besides, the more he spoke the more he sounded like a scolded child. He had come into the office too upset to form a rational argument, and he was coming across horribly. Coming into work was a mistake.

"Sandra, is there something you would like to add?" Barney asked when Alex stopped talking.

"I believe the problem is that Karen's definition of Alex's job, and my definition are completely different," Sandra said. "Alex needs to have an understanding of exactly what his role is and work to capacity in that role."

"Alex?" Barney said, prompting Alex to reply.

"My role is to run my team and see my projects successfully reach the market on time and on budget," Alex said.

"No. That's my job. Your job is to analyze opportunities," Sandra said. "To provide documentation and source materials to me as needed."

So it was a demotion then. She was basically telling him that his job was going to be the same as Elissa's. "That is not the most efficient use of my skills and abilities."

"Regardless of what you think your skills and abilities are, you are sorely mistaken," Sandra said. "Karen may have let you think you could work above your station, but I most certainly will not."

"Work above my station?" Alex scoffed. "I run one of the most successful teams in this company. My team handles ten times as much as your other project managers."

"Which is also part of the problem," Sandra said. "You are stretched so thin that you make mistakes and overlook them."

"I don't make mistakes," Alex said.

"Alex, everyone makes mistakes," Barney replied.

"Sure, but I am thorough, analytical, and check and double check everything to make sure its perfect," Alex said.

"If that was the case I would not have found so many problems with your documents," Sandra said.

"Your problems were just differences of opinions. There was absolutely nothing wrong with my projects."

"Alex, we're not being confrontational," Barney cautioned.

As if this whole setup was not designed to be confrontational.

"We are going to begin retraining you with fundamentals," Sandra said. "Your inability to provide what is required shows me that you need to learn what the true expectations are."

"Are we getting back to your request for *questions*?" Alex asked.

"You did not give me what was expected to run the meeting," Sandra said.

"You asked for questions. I gave you questions. If you wanted an agenda, issues log, and all that other crap you should have requested it."

"As a project manager you should have been aware that I needed it and that was what I was looking for."

"I'm not a mind reader," Alex said bitterly.

"Alex," Barney cautioned.

"I'm sorry, but this is ridiculous. I wasn't here to run the meeting. The person who facilitates either prepares materials or has someone prepare them for him. When I am here I prepare everything I need or have Elissa or Junador put it together for me. If Sandra was running the meeting she should have made sure she had everything she needed or asked someone for assistance."

"I did. I asked you," Sandra said.

"Yeah, well, when it's me, I always look over what Elissa or Junador give me and approve it before sending the materials out. If you didn't like what I prepared you should have said something long before the meeting. Who is really the one that is negligent here? Me? Or you?"

"Do you see what I deal with?" Sandra asked, rolling her eyes.

"Alex, we're trying to be cordial," Barney said.

"Trust me, I am being cordial. You wouldn't want to see how upset I really am and what I really want to say," Alex said.

"You obviously need to adjust your attitude, accept what your job really is, and learn how to do it properly."

"I have never received a single complaint about my work before you," Alex said.

"You must not be listening," Sandra replied. "I hear complaints about you all the time. Frankly I'm amazed Karen put up with you like this as long as she had."

"Who is complaining? What are the complaints?" Alex demanded, wanting to defend himself against his so-called accusers.

"I'm not going to get into that, but I hear it all the time," Sandra said.

"I want details," Alex said.

"Alex, the details are not important," Barney said.

"Like hell they're not!" Alex shouted. "I don't believe a word that is coming out of her mouth. If people, other than her, are really complaining about me, I want to hear it."

"Let's move on," Barney said.

"I have reallocated your projects," Sandra said.

"Woah, wait a minute, what?"

"You cannot handle as many projects as you have. Your position also does not call for a team. While you have been away I have split up your projects to various managers and reassigned the various teams accordingly. You will do your job based on my definition of it, not Karen's."

"Excuse me?"

Sandra slid a piece of paper across the desk. "This is the new breakdown."

Alex glanced down. He had three projects left under his name, two small ones with no real responsibility at all, and his one big online game—at least she wasn't taking his baby away from him.

"You will also continue to represent our department in the status calls as we previously discussed," Sandra said.

Alex did not know how he could successfully represent the migration when he no longer was going to have his hands in all of the projects. He would need people to provide him with weekly status updates and report on those, rather than having first hand information.

Alex looked at Barney. "You're signing off on this?"

"We think it's for the best," Barney said.

Alex looked at the list again. Elissa had her own projects—six of them he noted—as did Sayuri. He actually had the fewest projects now of them all. Even Theresa and some of the other project managers were taking over what had been his. Junador was not listed at all.

"What will Junador's role be? Is he taking over as support?" Alex asked.

"Your role does not give you resources for support," Sandra said. "Elissa has been held back by your methods of running things."

"Alex, Junador was let go," Barney said.

"Excuse me?" Alex asked.

"We received complaints about him, too," Sandra said. "He was always asking the same questions over and over, wasting valuable time and resources. We felt that it was in our best interests to end his contract with us."

You know what they say about people in glass houses, Alex thought. "You should not have let someone from my team go without consulting me."

"He was on my team!" Sandra shrieked, her face growing red again. "You do not have a team! Everyone is on my team!"

"Alex, she is right," Barney said. "Karen isn't here anymore. Regardless of how things were before, Sandra is your manager now, and you were working at a level considerably higher than what you are supposed to be. We'll get everything back to normal, a slight adjustment period, and then I'm sure you'll see that everything is for the best."

Not likely, Alex thought. If there was one thing he hated—more than Sandra, that is—it was not being busy. He needed to be busy. He needed to be in control of what was going on. The thought of three projects and that's it drove him mad. Projects had periods of ups and downs where you were insanely busy or had nothing at all. What would he do in the down times with nothing to do? Managing projects like he had he always juggled them and filled in the gaps. But now what? Read some off-season articles about the Red Sox and roster moves? How was *that* a good use of his time for the company?

"Are we through?" Alex asked, ready to leave and not come back until Monday. He actually wasn't sure he even wanted to come in Monday, but until he and Crystal had a chance to talk he wasn't going to do anything rash.

"We're good here," Barney said. "I think this was productive. We're all on the same page now. Fantastic. Have a good weekend."

Alex got up, walked out of the conference room, and left the office without stopping at his desk. The same page? He didn't think that was possible. He would never see eye to eye with Sandra. This new arrangement wouldn't work, either. He could feel that deep down in his bones. But he had been ambushed and came off looking like the troublemaker. He had to think things through and deal with Sandra more rationally from this point on. He could not let her win. He could not let her control him. One of them would die before he let that happen.

15

Alex could not believe how badly things had turned out. He thought going to work after the convention to confront Sandra would somehow be a positive thing. That it would be like a burden lifted from him. But instead things were worse. In one meeting he had lost everything—his projects, his team, his responsibility, his respect. He did not know how he could possibly even face the rest of his former team after that. He was nothing now. Less than nothing. After all of his hard work, after all of his efforts, after all of the pushing to drive his success, he wound up with nothing.

He decided to take the back roads home. He normally would go route nine or hop on the Mass Pike if he was in a rush, but he needed some time to think and calm down before he saw Crystal. If he saw her like this, he did not think he could keep himself composed. He was always so strong, so confident, so self-assured, and now he was taken down and turned into a glorified secretary. Is that what a MIT and Harvard education got you? The ability to draft agendas and minutes for someone else who had inferior intellect to review and criticize?

"Fuck her," he growled under his breath as he pushed his foot down harder on the accelerator. Even on the winding back roads he was driving as if he were on the highway. His speedometer kept increasing—thirty, forty, fifty, sixty, seventy. The curves were coming like blurs and he took them by driving on the inside of each curve regardless of what side of the road it was on. If a car was on the other side facing him they would both likely die in a head-on collision, but he did not even consider that. He was too angry to think about anything other than accelerating faster and doing something that got his adrenaline pumping.

It had been too long since Alex had done something adventurous. He needed to get away, to be free, to reclaim his spirit and the fire that burned inside of his soul. He was too focused on his work and his job. Work was not life, just a means to an end, yet he had allowed it to consume him. He had allowed her too much power over him. That had to stop.

If he only had three projects, then there was no need for him to go to work early and leave late. There was not enough work to even fill an eight hour day. He would still go to work, but he would be just like everyone else who came and went like clockwork. Hell, he might even sleep in a little and come late. What would she know? She came in after him. Bitch probably had spies who would rat him out. But what did he care?

Maybe part of his problem with her was the fact that he did care so much. If he stopped caring, then maybe seeing her waddle, hearing her laugh, looking at her damned pink ink all over everything he did would not bother him so much. At least he would be home earlier, be able to spend more time with Crystal. If he looked at it that way, maybe everything would be okay.

Just as he knew he would stop working late as a form of rebellion—giving Sandra his absolute minimum effort, which, if he admitted it, was still working at a higher degree than most of the other project managers which he thought was pathetic—he also knew that he would never stop caring. Sandra would continue to upset him. He would not give in and just do things her way. Being a glorified secretary was not why he went to work every day. Sure, he would get paid the same to do less, but he needed more. He would rather work more and get paid less than get paid more and do less. That was just him.

Alex hit an open stretch with an intersection. He was doing eighty-five as he approached it. He saw headlights of another car and thought little of them until they pulled out in front of him. Alex's eyes widened and he jammed his foot on the brake, swerving and fishtailing as he tried to come to a stop. The vehicle in front of him then drove on, braking as if trying to get hit.

"What the fuck!" Alex growled. He glared at the car in front of him. All of his anger at Sandra and the meeting with Barney was shifted to this person who dared to cut him off and make him slow down. He had been thinking, finally seeing things clearly, and now this person dared to get in front of him.

Alex accelerated again and got right on the back of the other car. He glanced down at his speedometer and saw that he was only doing twenty-five. Even then the car in front of him applied their brake as they were taking the next curve.

"Un-fucking believable," Alex growled. As they rounded the curve and had a straight the car accelerated slightly, but then applied the brakes again. "Come on! Speed up you fuck! Look at all of that road ahead of you!"

Obviously the brake lights glaring in his face was a sign that the driver did not hear his shouts. Alex pounded on his horn, but the car only braked again and ignored him. With that not working he began flashing his high beams. He hoped the person would just get out of the way and let him go again. But in reply he saw the brake lights come on again.

"What the fuck is your problem! Get out of the way!" he shouted as he jammed his foot on the accelerator to give himself a burst of speed and got right up to the bumper of the car in front of him. He honked again and again and grinned as the car finally began to accelerate, but not nearly enough to satisfy him.

Alex saw the next curve in the road and decided he would pass on the inside, flying right by the car in the opposite lane. He waited for it, then moved his steering wheel in a quick jerk into the lane of oncoming traffic and jammed his foot on the accelerator. He pulled up parallel to the other car and risked a glance over, glaring at the other driver. Then he saw light in his peripheral vision and turned back in time to see an oncoming vehicle. Alex jammed his foot on the brake and swerved back into his lane as a pick-up truck soared past going the other direction, the driver's hand glued to the horn as it blared in protest.

"Shit!" Alex barked. He was not deterred though. He jammed his foot on the accelerator again and got right on the back of the car in front of him, and then turned his high beams on and left them on as he honked several times.

The car in front of him began to accelerate and not apply the brakes so much. They moved up to thirty, then forty, and then fifty. It was still not fast enough for Alex and he did not drop back. Regardless of the speed of the driver in front of him he matched it, staying inches from the car in front of him.

Even though he only went this way from time to time, he knew this road, the turns, and how dark it was. Part of the whole initiative to go green and conserve energy had street lights dimmed and working at only partial power. Most streets were darker and harder to see. This one only had a few lights to begin with—an infrequently used road with little need for that much use of precious energy. Alex took the curves knowing what to expect. The car in front of him must not have had the same knowledge as Alex saw them skidding around the curves, the back end of the car almost striking the barriers or trees.

If he was in his right frame of mind, he would recognize that the driver was not capable of maintaining such a pace. If he was in his right frame of mind he would recognize that with him tailgating as close as he was the driver could not even pull over and let him pass. If he was in his right frame of mind he would never display such reckless road rage and aggressiveness while driving. But he was not in his right frame of mind.

Alex kept accelerating, coming close to striking the car, then jamming his foot on the brake, then accelerating again. Every time he did he saw that the other car had accelerated to—now he was able to get up to sixty. He passed a speed limit sign and snorted at the twenty-five mile per hour speed limit sign followed by the dangerous curve sign. Such mundane limits were not for him. Just like being a glorified secretary for that bitch was not for him.

Thinking of Sandra was the wrong thing to do. He began screaming at the top of his lungs, letting out his anger and fury, and then began shouting at the car in front of him again, "Get the fuck out of my way!"

Then, without warning, the car was out of his way. Alex knew the steep turn and knew that the signs were warning about it, but the car in front went straight, off the road, into the trees. It struck doing sixty with so much force that Alex could hear the grinding of metal even inside his own vehicle. He watched as the car bounced, plowed into a tree, flipped over, and landed upside down with the tires still spinning.

He knew he should feel responsible. He knew he should feel bad about what happened. He knew he should stop to make sure everyone was okay. He knew he should dial 911 and ask for help. But instead, all he could do was smirk. "Serves you right for cutting me off."

As he accelerated and took the steep curve, leaving the car behind, he saw a flickering and glanced in his rearview mirror and saw that the car had caught on fire. As he finished the turn the other car and the fate of the driver was already forgotten. His part in the accident was not even a concern. His mind returned to Sandra, to his hatred of her, to how she had found a way to destroy his life, and how he had to find something to do about it.

16

Alex pulled into his driveway, turned the car off, and sat there staring at the wheel for a minute. He looked up at the house and saw Crystal inside one of the windows sitting and watching television. He took a deep breath and tried to push everything with Sandra out of his mind. He had not seen his wife for a week. He did not want to come home and have her see him upset and sulking.

He glanced at the mirror and tried to smile. It looked so fake. He tried again with the same results. Sighing he got out of the car, took his suitcase from the trunk and walked to the front door. He closed his eyes, breathed in and out several times, and then opened up the door up.

He heard the television shut off and saw Crystal running to him. He dropped his suitcase as she jumped into his arms, knocking him back a step into the door of the closet in the front foyer.

"I missed you so much!" she said as she began kissing his forehead, his cheek, and his mouth. "Welcome home!"

"I missed you, too," Alex said as he tightened his grip around her and leaned in for a kiss, finding her lips and letting the passion of the moment—the reunion—take away his issues with Sandra for the moment. He did not have to fake his smile with Crystal while they were kissing. He did not have to pretend. He just let his primal instincts take over. He was a man, she was a woman, they loved and wanted each other. That was enough for the moment.

Alex, with Crystal still straddling him, kicked the door closed behind him while he was still kissing her. He wondered if he should walk her up to the bedroom, or to the couch, or let her down and take her hand and lead her somewhere. But none of that worked for him. He wanted her here, now. He just kept kissing her harder and harder, with more fervor and longing.

"Someone missed me," Crystal said between kisses, but she was lost to the moment, too.

Alex turned them around, putting her back up against the closet door, and then used the leverage to free his hands. He reached for her top and pulled with all of his might, popping the buttons and exposing her to him. Her eyes showed a slight sign of shock, but then a longing as intensely as his. She liked it.

She reached over and did the same to him, tearing at his

button down shirt, the tie still fastened around his neck. She then untied that as he leaned in to kiss her breasts. He could not wait any longer. He had to have her. He needed to have her.

Crystal unwrapped her legs from around him and stood on the ground. As she did she began fumbling with his belt, unclasping it and then tugging at his pants. Once she had the button and zipper free, she pulled them down to his knees and then used her feet to push them the rest of the way down. With his pants off Crystal slid her hands into her own pants—sweatpants since she was home and wanted to be comfortable—and slid both those and her panties off.

As soon as they were down Alex was upon her again, kissing her neck passionately, his hands probing, feeling, examining the body he knew so well but had not been able to touch for a week. She jumped up, straddling him again, and then he entered her and they became one. He heard her gasp with each thrust as her back slammed against the closet door. He did not want her to be in pain. He moved away from the door, making sure he did not fall out of her, and put his arms behind her so that it would be him who would take the brunt of the blows.

"Don't stop," she whispered as she licked his ear.

Alex did not stop. He did as she asked, going harder and faster. He could hardly control himself and he did not want to. He felt his climax building and thought briefly about resisting it so that he was not the only one who got something out of it, but the primal urge pushed him forward and he moaned as his body trembled and he released the buildup.

Everything was sensitive. He slowed down but did not want to stop. He wanted her to be happy too. He looked into her eyes and saw her smiling back at him. Through his deep breaths he could hear her breathing just as deeply.

"Welcome home," she said as she leaned in to kiss him and then lowered her legs again.

"I can keep going," he protested.

"We have all night," Crystal said. She took his hand and then led him up to the bedroom. Alex went with her, only wanting to think about their reunion, to think about her, about them. Nothing else mattered. Nothing else existed.

Crystal brought them into the bedroom and slid into bed. Alex followed her in. She waited until he put the covers over them and then she snuggled into him, her fingers playing with the hair on his chest.

"How was the trip?"

"Long," he said. "I missed you."

"I can tell," Crystal said as she leaned over and kissed him again. "Did you go to work tonight?"

Alex winced at the comment. He should have called her. His flight landed hours ago. "I'm sorry, I should have called and let you know."

"That's okay, Sayuri called to tell me you might be late."

"She did?"

"She said you had some things you needed to get off your chest," Crystal added. "Is everything okay now?"

Alex sighed. He did not want to think about this now. He only wanted to feel the warmth of her body, the tenderness of her touch.

"Alex, you can tell me. What happened?"

"I wanted to confront Sandra," Alex said. "To defend my team, myself. To find some way to make her stop this agenda she has of tearing my team apart."

"What happened?"

"She practically ambushed me," Alex sighed. "She and Barney pulled me into a conference room. Nothing was her, it was all me. My problems. My inability to adapt. My inadequacies with being a project manager."

"Inadequacies?" Crystal laughed. "Have they read your reviews? After everything you've done for that company they call you inadequate! I hope you resigned right then and there."

"No," Alex admitted. "Maybe I should have."

"You definitely should have," Crystal replied. "There is no reason for them to treat you this way. You give your heart and soul to that company."

"Yeah," Alex agreed. "At least I did. Not anymore."

"No?"

"No. I made that decision driving home," Alex said.

"What led you to that? What did Sandra and Barney say?"

"That Sandra's definition of my role is different from the job I was doing or how Karen saw it. That I was supposed to take notes, write drafts of minutes, and prepare materials for her."

"Seriously?"

"Seriously," Alex said. "She basically told me that I was to be a glorified secretary."

"No way," Crystal said, growing upset herself. "Not you. Just quit. You'll find something better. We can handle the single salary for a while."

"My father didn't raise a quitter," Alex said, then speaking in a tone as closely to his father as he could, "Come on Alex, keep going, an Adams never quits."

"Sometimes it's for the best," Crystal said.

"I'll think about it," Alex replied. "I honestly don't know how I'll face everyone Monday."

"Why?"

"They aren't my team anymore. Sandra took the team away. She also took all of my projects away and left me with just three."

"Three projects?" Crystal scoffed. "You'll be bored out of your mind."

"I agree," Alex said. "Can you believe that she gave Elissa more projects than me?"

"Really?"

"Apparently it's just me she doesn't like, not anyone else from my team," Alex said. "Lucky me. Oh, and you'll love this... she says that she receives complaints about me all the time. I've never heard complaints. In fact, Karen used to forward me emails from people we worked with who commended how quickly I got the business, how thorough I was, and how I exceeded their every expectation."

"I think she's just saying that to get to you."

"I agree," Alex admitted. "If someone other than her had a problem, I'm sure I would have heard about it by now."

"So what are you going to do?"

"Be the average employee she wants me to be," Alex said as he exhaled. "I'll hate every minute of it, but once my promotion goes through hopefully I'll get my team back."

"When is that going to happen?"

"I don't know. Good question."

"You should ask Barney about it," Crystal suggested.

"Yeah, I should," Alex agreed. "I'll talk to him Monday and see how all of this effects that."

"What happens when you get it?"

"I'm thinking about looking for a position on another team within the company. Someplace where I can build my own team again. Most of my people would probably come with me. Think of how Sandra would be then when her most effective people all begin transferring out of Fantasy and over to Science Fiction or children's animation or something."

"Would they go?"

"Some," Alex said. "Elissa would go wherever I went."

"Even if Sandra is taking her under her wing and giving her more responsibility?" Crystal asked.

"I would think so," Alex said. "I would hope so. But even if she didn't, I'll find my team again."

Crystal leaned in and kissed him. "I know you will. I have faith. But if this doesn't work, remember that you can leave."

"I know, thank you," he said.

She kissed him again, and this time they did not stop, allowing their passion and desire sweep through them again. Unlike at the door, this time was more intimate, more tender, it lasted longer, and it left both of them feeling fulfilled.

17

For the rest of the weekend Alex did not think about work at all. He and Crystal had breakfast in bed, then went out dancing Saturday night. On Sunday they went for a brunch buffet and then spent the afternoon relaxing and cuddling in each other's arms. It was so nice and peaceful just being together and only caring about the person who they loved.

Crystal suggested that they find some time to themselves and get away. Alex agreed. He rarely took time off from work because he was always so busy, but if he was to be a glorified secretary, then it seemed pointless to put the company first. By the time the weekend was done they had plotted a trip north to Canada to see some sights and then back down to Maine for some white water rafting.

Crystal said that she had some friends who were interested in going, and she spoke to them and arranged for an entire group to meet for the final portion of the trip and rented a cabin for the rafting trip. It would have some time for them to be alone, but then end it with a group of friends and some fun. She knew Alex would love the rafting part the most, and since they would wind up stuck with people they did not know if it was just the two of them, why not have eight people.

Alex had to clear it at work, but doubted that Sandra would have a problem with him not being there. She probably would prefer him being out of the office as much as possible. If she did have a problem, then he would just call in sick each day of the trip. Let her fire him. He didn't care anymore.

At one point during the weekend he was flipping through the newspaper and found a picture of a burnt car and an article about reckless driving on windy-back-roads resulting in the death of two teenagers. The article then went on to question whether the age teenagers were able to get licenses should be pushed back until they were more responsible and older. There was no reference of another vehicle, only the one that lost control.

Alex put the paper aside, not wanting to think about the two teenagers or how crazed he was driving home Friday night. It was best not to think about it. After all, there was nothing he could do about it now. If he allowed himself to beat himself up over it, all that would accomplish is gaining a guilty conscience. He equated that to weakness.

On Sunday night he asked Crystal if she wanted to head down to the range and squeeze off a few rounds. He knew she only got her license to carry and fired guns because it was something he enjoyed. But she agreed to go.

They had searched clubs extensively when they first decided to get memberships. One was an outdoor club that seemed too restrictive. One was an indoor club and you couldn't shoot rifles at all. The one they wound up with had an indoor and outdoor range, as well as a rifle range that allowed you to shoot every 200 yards beginning at 200 yards out and extending to 1000 yards.

Alex was quite pleased with their pick. The indoor portion of the club had twenty lanes with the pulleys to allow a target to be as close as you wanted it or up to fifty feet away. Even with twenty lanes, he had never seen anyone else shooting regardless of when he had gone. It did not matter if it was day, night, weekday, or weekend. He was always alone at the club.

As members they had twenty-four-hour access and keys to get into the front gate and all buildings. Alex drove and stopped at the gate. He got up, unlocked the gates, drove in, then went back and closed the gate and locked it behind him. The club was on private property and they were very serious about making sure trespassers never got in—liability issues and all. Everyone who had a firearms license had to take a gun safety course. Before getting a club membership everyone had to go through a series of safety protocol classes to make sure they were aware of the dangers of being around a place where guns were used—just think about the person who did not realize someone was shooting at 1000 yards and walked into the 400 yard area. But someone who was not a member would not have the benefit of those lessons and could get seriously hurt. Everyone took safety very seriously.

Since it was night Alex did not even consider the rifles. He brought a variety of handguns for them to shoot, ranging from a .22 caliber revolver to a .45 caliber semi-automatic. They had enough ammunition on them to stay here for several hours, though they probably would only shoot enough for an hour or two.

Alex used his key to unlock the door of the main building and extended his arm to prompt Crystal to walk in first. Once inside he turned on the lights and led her down the ramp to the area where the range was. Usually there were targets laid out for them to take, but he did not see any.

"Give me a minute and I'll check the supply closet," Alex said.

"Okay, I'll get us set up," Crystal said, taking the handbag from him and pulling the cases of guns out, unlocking them, and setting them down for them to use.

Alex walked back into the main room and used another key to unlock the supply closet. He stepped in and saw all manners of tools to help with the upkeep of the grounds, including lawn mower, rake, shovel, saw, axe, screwdrivers, and dozens of assorted tools. Walking past them he found a shelf with targets on it. He took a handful of them, backed out of the closet, closed the door, and locked it.

"I got some," he said as he walked over to Crystal by the range. He examined her handiwork and saw that the guns were out already with the appropriate ammunition placed next to each one. "What do you want to start with?"

"The .45," she said with a grin.

"That'ta girl," Alex said. Most women he knew would begin with the smaller .22 caliber, but not Crystal. She went for the biggest handgun with the most kick—and she knew how to use it.

Alex had never taken a class as a kid. He knew they had things like junior shooting leagues and tournaments and competitions. But his father had taught him how to shoot and even without the hours and hours of practice he was consistently accurate and competent with a firearm. He had taught Crystal himself and had always been impressed with how quickly she had picked up on it.

There were a few matches he entered over the years. Nothing serious or consistent, but the club had monthly matches and if he had some down time he would go down and participate. Even there he always shot in the top five, usually in the top three. Since there averaged fifty shooters who shot regularly and competed monthly, he was quite pleased with his results. But he would not be totally satisfied until he was the best and claimed the club trophy. He was close, but not quite yet—the match required not just accuracy but speed, and while he had the accuracy down pat he could not combine the two as much as needed to be to take home the championship. Not yet, at least.

As they shot he tried to work on speed a bit. He emptied clips and put another one in and continued shooting without pause. The faster he got the less accurate he found himself. He preferred the accuracy. Seeing misses really bothered him.

He and Crystal stayed for a couple of hours and then decided to call it a night. They took the targets they shot and brought them with them. He knew they would wind up in a trash can sooner or later, but they always seemed to keep their targets for a little while to show how good they did. They packed up and locked the guns and remaining ammunition, turned off all of the lights and locked the main building, and locked and secured the gate when they went through.

While driving home, Crystal leaning over and cuddling into his right arm, Alex felt more calm than he had in a long time. But it was Sunday, and that meant work was looming. Just a handful of hours and he would be faced with Sandra again. He did not want to ruin his calm and tried not to think about it. But the thought was there. It was inevitable. Sandra would be back to tear him down again. Something had to be done. Something soon.

18

Alex dreaded going to work Monday morning. But he got up, showered, dressed, and left with just enough time to make it for the start of his shift and not any earlier like he normally did. He stopped and chatted with Bob for awhile at security as if nothing was different or wrong, and then went up to his desk.

He sat down, logged into his computer, and saw over four hundred emails waiting for him—the downside of being away for a week. Normally he would go through each, picking a project at a time and going through the entire week. Now he wondered how exactly he should do it. Should he focus on his three projects and ignore the others? Just forward them to the new project manager? He balked at that thought. He would answer them as if he was still running the projects and copy the new project manager.

Let them take it from there.

Before he began though he sent a quick email request to Sandra for a week off in May for the trip be and Crystal discussed. It would be his first vacation of the year. He checked the vacation calendar and saw that nobody else had requested it off. He pointed that out in his request. He did, however, note that Sandra was on vacation for a couple of weeks in April. At least then he would potentially have things back to normal for a time. He could hardly wait.

With the request sent he went through his email looking at the meeting requests first and approved all of those to update his calendar. He then began looking at email chains to catch up and added his feedback and insights where appropriate. He knew Sandra would probably be upset with him for still commenting on his old projects, but he wasn't thinking about her—his team, or his former team, still needed answers, and whether she realized it or not he was a key resource.

After the emails began flowing through the network people began showing up at his desk. Doug, Steven, and Damien all stopped by from development. Sharon and Garret from the concept team came by. Sabrina from marketing actually asked him if he wanted to go to breakfast to talk about it. Even Sayuri's Japanese team all stopped by with words of encouragement and comments about how he was being treated dishonorably.

Everton and Elissa were the last two to come over. They

did not want to talk to him at his desk like the others. They wanted to see him more privately. Sayuri caught them as they were walking to a room that was on the wing opposite from where their offices were so Sandra would not see them meeting. Sayuri joined them as well.

"That's a right dastardly thing she did," Everton said. "I don't like the way things are turning out at all."

"That makes two of us," Alex said. "But at this point I see few options."

"If it's any consolation, my team has already agreed to stop working overtime," Everton said. "They'll do their best during normal hours, but we all refuse to stay late and go that extra step to make aggressive deadlines. In fact, all of our timeline projections will have to be reprioritized and the dates pushed out."

"Don't do that," Alex said. "We still have product to get out and a merger to see successfully completed."

"It's out of my hands, lad," Everton shrugged. "My people refuse to work for that bloody witch."

"What do you want us to do?" Elissa asked.

"Do your jobs the way I know you can," Alex said. "She thinks all of you are tainted because you worked with and for me. Prove to her that you're all as great as I know you are."

"Our loyalty is to you," Elissa said.

"Then work for her as if you were working for me," Alex replied.

"It's a raw deal," Everton replied, shaking his head. "Not right at all."

"I can't argue with you, but that's the way it is. At least for now," Alex said.

"Did you want me to speak to my father?" Sayuri asked. "He thinks very fondly of you."

"No. Whatever happens, I need to fight my own battles."

"You're a stand up chap, Alex," Everton said. "I hope things get back to normal soon. I'll miss working with you."

"Me too," Alex admitted. "Now we should all get back to work before someone notices that we're gone." Everyone knew that "someone" was Sandra. Nobody else would care if some of the most productive employees in the company were in a short meeting together.

Alex was sincerely touched by all of the support that he got. It also made him even more certain that Sandra was lying about people complaining about him. His people would not show such admiration and support if deep down they were glad he was brought back to reality and taken down a few pegs. No, she had her own agenda and she was pursuing it.

As they walked back to their desks Alex saw Barney in his office. He decided that a quick chat would be beneficial. He knocked on the door and stepped into the office. "You got a minute?"

"Come in," Barney said, waving for him to enter.

Alex stepped into the office and closed the door behind him. The next words he knew had to be careful. He believed everything he had said on Friday. There was nothing he regretted saying. But his reputation with the company and his professionalism was on the line.

"I wanted to apologize for the way I handled the meeting Friday." It wasn't bad. He didn't apologize for lashing out at Sandra or his animosity toward her. Only the fact that he lost his temper.

"Think nothing of it," Barney said. "There are times people are in the heat of the moment and say things that they don't mean. Let's just pretend that Friday never happened."

"I would like that, thank you," Alex said.

"Is there anything else?" Barney asked.

"Actually, there is," Alex said. "I would never ask for this, even when Karen had first brought it up, but in light of my new role and my desire to be back in a position where I can run projects again, I was wondering if there was any word on my promotion?"

Barney frowned at the question, he averted his eyes, as if he did not want to look at Alex. "Unfortunately Karen is not here anymore."

"Before she left she told me the paperwork was in and the promotion was still going through," Alex said, clinging on to that hope.

"Well, that's normally true, but Sandra is your new manager now. She has to sign off on the promotion since Karen left the company. Until she does, I'm afraid the promotion is not going to go through."

Alex tightened his hands into fists. After apologizing for his behavior he certainly was not going to allow his temper to get the better of him now. If Sandra was the one who had the fate of his promotion in her hands, then there was no way in hell he was going to get his promotion.

"I see," Alex said.

"I wish there was something that I could do," Barney replied. "But my hands are tied. My best advice is to try to get on the same page with Sandra. Learn from her, see what her style is like, try to be her friend or something. You always seem really good at getting even the most difficult people to open up to you. This should be no different."

Alex had no faith that he would ever manage to accomplish that with Sandra. "One more thing. I intend to do as you and Sandra want, and do my job to the best of my ability, even if it is with this radically reduced role. But I know I can do so much more. You need manager approval to look for other opportunities in the company. I do not believe Sandra would give it to me. Will you?"

"Do you really think leaving the team is the best option?" Barney asked.

"I will try, I honestly will, but I do not believe that that woman and I will ever be able to coexist in the same space. That being said, it's better to move on and explore other alternatives. With my efforts on the merger I have quite a reputation and image built up. I think I can get something," Alex explained. "Also, unless you get a three or above on a performance appraisal, you are not allowed to post for other positions. I have always gotten fours and fives. I have no faith that I will come anywhere close to that if Sandra reviews me and that goes into my permanent record."

"I wouldn't be so sure about that," Barney said.

Alex couldn't believe how blind he was. "Regardless, this gives me some time, but I will not still be in this position at the end of the year so that Sandra's evaluation can follow me around the company. I will either find another position within the company or I will tender my resignation and move on."

"I would hate to lose you," Barney said. "But I understand. You have to be comfortable coming to work, and obviously you're not. I'll give you permission to look, but pray that you'll find a way to remain and be productive here. This is where you belong."

"Thanks Barney," Alex said. "I'll keep you in the loop with whatever happens."

"I appreciate that."

Alex thanked him again, opened the door and walked back to his desk. As he did so he saw Sandra glaring at him. The fact that Alex felt comfortable talking to her boss probably irritated her more than anything. He was not surprised to find a new email pop up five minutes later rejecting his vacation request. She did not explain her reasoning, she just said no.

19

The next few weeks were agonizing. Alex hated having very little to do, and that was exactly what he had. He also was never one to slow down and take a long time on something. He didn't want to make a document last. He had his own standards to adhere to, which he had to admit were often quite loftier than the expectations put upon him. But he would not reduce his own productivity and efforts just to drag something out.

Even with his reduced role things did not improve with Sandra. She was critical of everything he did, was quick to put him down, demanded to see him for almost everything he did and told him how horrible he was doing or the fact she could not believe he was doing something she did not want him to. She never gave him the opportunity to speak or defend himself. She just attacked and lashed out.

The worst was his big project—his baby. He got a call from Koichi Takato with a request for an urgent meeting to go over some pertinent developments. Koichi had spoken directly with Creative Visions CEO Brett Curran, and when Alex followed up with Brett he sent Alex a list of key participants that he wanted involved in a joint call with Japan. Alex was quite pleased to see that Brett did not put Sandra on the list of participants. Since he was the CEO, as far as Alex was concerned, he would get the people he wanted and needed and Sandra could stay as far away from this as possible—the further the better. For the first time in weeks he felt like his old self again. He loved it.

Alex reviewed the list of attendees Brett submitted and suggested a couple of people that were not on it—people from his old team who had been instrumental in getting the game to the point it was at. Brett agreed with the additions. The call was to be set up for 8:00 at night so that the Tokyo participants could call in during their mornings.

Alex booked the room with video conferencing and sent out the invites to the people Brett originally specified and also those he agreed to add. Alex was expected to kick the meeting off, but then it would be Brett and Tomiro who would take the lead from there. Sayuri was also on the list and would be present in the States for the call.

On the day of the meeting Sandra found out about it. To say she exploded was an understatement. She walked over to his desk, said she wanted to see him, and then walked into a conference room and closed the door behind her. Alex did not know what she wanted to see him about, but found out quickly enough.

Her face was even more red and flushed than he had ever seen it. Her eyes were practically bulging out. Her whole body was tense and trembling with fury. Then she began shrieking at him on the top of her lungs.

"How dare you set up a meeting with Brett Curran and Tomiro Takato!"

"Brett asked..." that's as far as he got. He could not even defend himself.

"Don't you dare talk back to me! I've told you before that I am to be copied on all of your correspondence! Obviously you do not know how to follow instructions! If you fail to do so again, for *anything*, I will have disciplinary actions followed and have you put on probation and then fired!

"How dare you even think about talking to Brett Curran! It's my job to represent this division, not you!" she screamed. She then took several deep breaths, exhaling through her nose, glaring at him in disgust. She then added, "You are forbidden to go to that meeting!"

As she said it she stood, opened the door and let it slam into the wall, and stormed out.

"Forbidden?" Alex said, "What am I, a two-year old?"

He balled his hands into fists; shocked that she was that upset and would prevent him from going to a meeting that the CEO asked him to set up. It's not like he had purposefully excluded her. The CEO did. She was only mad at him because he had better contacts and networks than she did.

But what now? If he was forbidden to go to the meeting, what would Brett and Tomiro think? They both expected him there. It was his project. His baby. They knew that. What value would she bring to the project? Absolutely none.

Alex was half tempted to defy her and go anyway, but what good would that do him? It would just get her shrieking at him again and getting those so-called disciplinary actions started. If he was leaving he wanted to leave on his own terms, no hers.

He already had several interviews. There was one position for an Assistant Vice President that would have him run the local office and report in to a Vice President in Japan. That position was more favorable than the others. The emphasis was on military games, historical references, and all things combat related. The thought of having a boss half way across the world after dealing with Sandra was also quite alluring. He had an interview with someone in Human Resources, a phone interview with the person he would be reporting to in Japan as well as another Japanese manager, and an interview with a couple of Vice Presidents who were already in the states and had a sister-team here. All of the interviews had gone well. It would be just his luck to get involved in disciplinary actions and making him ineligible to move right when he was about to get an offer.

Alex decided to swallow his pride. He went back to his desk, ignored the looks of sympathy from people who heard Sandra shrieking at him and typed a quick message to Brett letting him know that his manager, Sandra, had indicated that she wished to represent the division in the meeting tonight. He wanted to add more, to say that if Brett had any questions he would be happy to address them, but he did not. He left it short, sweet, and simple. He did not want anything that Sandra could translate as him going behind her back again or disobeying her orders.

He left on time again that night, and while the meeting kicked off at night he was at home watching a movie with Crystal, cuddled together on the couch. He could not remember what the movie was. His mind was on the meeting and what he was missing. Or even worse, how Sandra might be tearing him down in front of the men who thought so highly of him.

There was nothing he could do though. At least not until he got the offer and was able to leave. Hopefully the offer came in soon. He needed to get away. He did not know how much longer he could put up with the way things were going.

20

During the meeting that Alex was forbidden to attend the decision was made to split the online multi-player Fantasy game into two releases. In order to beat the competition to market there was going to be an interim release that allowed people to play and level up to a certain point. If they reached that point then the game would essentially freeze and they would be stuck. Release two would pick things up from that point and continue to advance the game. Presuming that the development of the game was done successfully gamers should never be aware of the fact that the original code was incomplete.

In order to speed up production, there were other short cuts that were being discussed as well. Things like reducing the need for equipment, storage capacity, beasts of burden, and even a wide array of armor and weapons. Alex could not believe how much was coming out of his project for this new "interim solution" and how shortsighted it was. Even if they wanted to cut the code releases in half, to remove other things that had already been designed—features of the game that helped make it desirable and more realistic—they were removing the gamer appeal.

Further, even if the second patch plugged in the things that came out, the transition was supposed to be seamless. How was it seamless when something fundamental like the ability to carry supplies was removed, and then suddenly when you build up to a certain level you just miraculously get that feature added?

He hated the decisions being made without his feedback. The game he was designing was supposed to be epic. Instead it was no better than any normal console game on the market, just that people could play it online. He wondered how much of the proposed revisions came from Sandra.

He could not sit idly by. He responded to the email with details of the revisions to all participants with his thoughts and concerns and copied both Doug Malone and Everton Taylor. Doug responded a few minutes after expressing that the development time for such a proposal would double his team's timeline and that features being removed would not be feasible.

Naturally, when Sandra came in, she pulled him into a room and yelled at him again, telling him that it was not his place to express his opinions, only to draft up a new analysis document with the new requirements for the interim approach. She also sent out an email replying to all apologizing for Alex's comments and pointing out that he was not aware of the prior night's discussion—that frustrated him to no end. Here she was making it sound like he was being negligent when in reality it was her who forbade him from going to the meeting.

Over the next couple of weeks several things began happening. First, the stock market began declining as the market came to a near collapse. Words of recession were spoken on the news in whispers as companies began laying people off and unemployment was reaching record highs. Working for Sandra, Alex had little doubt that if a layoff were to happen that he would be a part of it. There was no way she would recommend that he remain on board. He definitely was not as valuable to Creative Strategists under her management style as he was just a few months before when he was on the top of the world.

But it was not the layoffs that bothered him the most. At least a layoff would give him a package deal and make him eligible for unemployment benefits while he looked for something else—something he admitted in this market would be a lot harder than it had been if he left when Crystal first urged him to do so. But what bothered him the most was the fact that Creative Visions and Takato Games had essentially implemented a hiring freeze, which cut his new Assistant Vice President job off as an option. The Japanese manager was flying in to the states to meet with Alex when the announcement was made and the job requisition was cancelled. The chance to leave Sandra, to get his promotion, and to be back to normal suddenly vanished in a heartbeat.

Along with the hiring freeze was the announcement that all raises and bonuses would also be frozen. Since those would not kick in until after the New Years he had awhile before that would impact him. But, if he was unable to leave the division internally, that meant Sandra would wind up reviewing him if he stayed—and an economy collapse was probably the wrong time to willingly walk away from a job. At Creative Visions raises and bonuses were direct percentages based upon the rating one received on their review. The higher the rating, the higher the payout. Obviously, even if there were raises and bonuses, Sandra would never give him his normal review rating. That was probably for the best then that there was nothing. At least her bad review would not impact him financially. All it would do is impact his ability to post if the hiring freeze was ended.

He did not like the outlook. In fact, he felt trapped. With all of Crystal's encouragement to leave, he had always felt like he had options to do so. He would apply and look for something else without leaving—no use risking a hardship while doing a job search. But now it would b virtually impossible to find something else. If he could not get away from Sandra internally, or externally, then he was stuck with her, and that was not something he thought he could come to terms with.

Secondly, Sandra took her vacation as planned. Alex thought that for once he would be free of her influence and could run things the way he thought they should be run without her looking over his shoulder and criticizing him for everything. For the first time in a long time he thought about how much he could legitimately accomplish while she was gone.

Doug Malone wanted a meeting to discuss the new interim approach to the online role playing game. He felt that they could cut the game in half without removing features and that it would be ready to be released four months earlier than if they removed them. The concern then was whether the added features would take up the additional four months in testing because there was more that might not work properly.

Alex set up the meeting to discuss. Since Sandra was on vacation he did not include her in the invite—after all, she wasn't here so why would she need to be invited? Instead he optionally invited Barney so that in Sandra's absence her boss was aware of the meeting in the event that Sandra did not feel that Alex could handle it on his own. He hated adding Barney, but he figured Sandra would be less likely to be upset by it.

Twenty minutes after the invite went out Barney sent

Alex an email indicating that he spoke with Sandra and that the meeting should be cancelled. Alex practically flipped out. He launched an email right back, indicating that business does not just come to a standstill because one person was out of the office. That he had invited Barney in lieu of Sandra which was perfectly acceptable and that he disagreed with the decision to delay. He then wrote about the concerns expressed and why there was urgency to have the meeting. He clicked send and stared at Barney's door.

After waiting a minute or two to make sure Barney had a chance to read it he got up and went into Barney's office to stress his case. Barney seemed quite receptive and agreed, but said he had to run it by Sandra for her perspective because he knew she wanted to be involved. An hour later he got an email with a simple "Please comply and cancel the meeting."

Alex did as instructed and went home early. What was the point of him even being there if he could not do anything while Sandra was out of the office? Obviously without her presence he was next to useless. She must have felt the same way, or at least felt that he was not needed in the office, because he got an approval to his request for a vacation that she had originally denied. At least she was letting him get away.

Third, one night without Sandra there he stayed at work until after 8:00 to dial in to one of the Tokyo calls. When the call was done and he went out to leave, his tires were all slashed and his windshield shattered. He sat there staring at his car for a long time, wondering who would do this to him. The only name that popped into his head was Sandra. It had to be her. She didn't have a life as far as he knew. She probably did not go anywhere on her vacation. She could have done it.

Sayuri, who also had stayed for the meeting, drove him home after the tow truck came and took his SUV away. Throughout everything she was most sympathetic. He was glad she was here. He knew he could talk to Crystal and she would be there for him, but Sayuri actually saw the way Sandra treated him and how it impacted him. No matter how much he explained things to Crystal, it was all second hand and stories. She just did not understand as well as Sayuri did.

Sayuri also had her own insight into the issue. She believed that Sandra was threatened by Alex. She knew how good he was, how much more education he had than her, how charismatic he was, and how he managed to get people to do more for him than anyone else ever could. She saw him as a rival who could take her position away from her and was reacting to that by trying to discredit him and tarnish his good name.

Before she brought him home they stopped off for some drinks to let him vent and talk about work. He did not know how many he had, and he would never use alcohol as an excuse, but the following morning he woke up in bed next to Sayuri, both naked and with the scent of sex all over them.

21

Alex stood in Sayuri's shower with the water pounding on him. He kept scrubbing and scrubbing but no matter how hard he scrubbed, he still felt dirty. He could not believe what happened between him and Sayuri. He loved his wife. He loved his marriage. He loved his life with his wife. Crystal was the perfect wife that any man would be envious to call his own and here he was cheating on her.

As he continued scrubbing he thought of Sandra and how she had driven him to this. She and all of her pressure, her antics. If she had not come in and tore his life apart the way she did none of this would have happened. Now what? Did he tell Crystal? Beg her for forgiveness? Or hide it from her? He spent the entire night out. How the hell did he cover that up?

And what about Sayuri? She was a good friend. A valued colleague. Would things be different between them now? She believed in honor. Would she expect him to divorce Crystal and marry her so as not to dishonor her family? Would she ever be able to be the same with him again?

He hated not knowing what to do. He hated the situation he was in. He hated what this meant for his life and his livelihood. Sandra just had a way to twist his mind and make him so angry that he could hardly control himself. He never would have cheated on Crystal if Sandra had not led him to it. How could he face his wife?

"Alex?"

Alex froze under the pounding water. He peered through the glass doors and saw Sayuri standing there in the bathroom. He was not sure what to say. Did not know what was appropriate. Feeling modest he shifted, using his leg to cover himself so she could not see. She actually giggled at that.

"I think it's a little late for modesty."

"Sayuri, please don't say that," Alex said with a sigh that spoke volumes.

"It is okay, Alex-san," Sayuri said. "I will make this very easy for you. You love Crystal. We both know that. I will cherish last night, getting to know you this way, but it was to fulfill a need, to help you through your pain, not under any delusion of true love or desire."

Was she at least letting him off the hook? Could he accept that? Obviously he and Sayuri had a connection. It went deeper than just her understanding of what he was going through with Sandra. He thought back and saw the signs along the way. It began with their trip to San Francisco and the massage. She had been gentle, caring, compassionate—everything he needed her to be other than his wife.

"Sayuri, I'm so sorry," Alex said.

"There is nothing to apologize for," Sayuri said. "I am glad I was able to be there for you. To be able to help you. I hope that this does not change that fact for you. I will always be there for you Alex-san. In whatever way you need."

That made it worse. She was willing to be the other woman just to help him if he needed it. She deserved so much more. So much better.

"You've been in there a long time," Sayuri said. "Why don't you come out. We'll have breakfast and then I'll drive you home."

Alex turned the knob of the shower and stepped out, grabbing a towel. Sayuri was in a simple Japanese silk robe. He hated the fact that looking at her like this made him want her again. What was happening to him? He was not the kind of guy who strayed, looked at other women, and wanted to have affairs. Yet here he was wanting to drop his towel and take Sayuri right here and right now. But he resisted the urge. He had to resist the urge.

Sayuri looked disappointed. He wondered if she had been able to see the desire in his eyes and wanted it to. But she then backed out of the bathroom. "I'll leave you be and fix us something to eat."

"Thanks," Alex said.

"You should call Crystal," Sayuri suggested. "Apologize for last night and let her know you'll be home soon."

"I don't know what to say," Alex said, lowering his eyes to the floor.

"She already knows you're here," Sayuri said.

"What?" Alex asked, shocked at that.

"When you fell asleep I called her and told her that you were sleeping on my couch," Sayuri said.

"Why did you do that?"

"I knew you would not want to hurt her or have problems," Sayuri said. For a moment she looked like she felt guilty. As if it was her actions and hers alone that jeopardized their happiness. "I told her something happened to your car, we went out for some drinks, you got rather sluggish and sleepy, and I didn't think I could make it all the way to your house and back. She was quite grateful that I took care of you."

"I... thank you. I appreciate that," Alex said.

Sayuri stepped back into the bathroom and leaned up and kissed him on the cheek. "I always have, and always will have your back, Alex-san."

As she walked out he hated how he imagined pulling her back, kissing her more passionately, and making love to her again. It was not just the alcohol last night. He really wanted her and she wanted him. Accepting that, he knew he would have to fight it. He could never allow this to happen again. He could not betray Crystal again. Both of them deserved better than he was capable of at the moment.

After his shower Alex got dressed. He only ate a little of the breakfast Sayuri prepared, wanting instead to just get home to Crystal. Until he was able to look her in the eye and see if he could talk to her without breaking down, he would not rest easily. Sayuri seemed to understand and hurried to get ready.

When they got to his house Sayuri went in with him. Alex wasn't sure if that was a good idea or not. He thought for sure they would look more guilty and she would see right through them. But Sayuri argued that Crystal would be more suspicious if she just dropped him off and left.

As he walked inside Crystal peered around the corner from the kitchen and smiled at him. "Had a little trouble last night I hear?"

"A little," Alex said. "Someone slashed all of my tires and caved the windshield in."

Crystal's smile faded. She walked over. "Does security know who it is?"

"I'll check with Bob," Alex said. "Hopefully he caught something on camera."

Crystal then looked at Sayuri. "Thanks again for taking care of him for me."

"It was my honor," Sayuri said with a slight bow.

"He definitely doesn't do well when he drinks too much, does he?"

"Not really," Sayuri said with a conspiratorial laugh.

Alex watched the two and wondered how they could laugh and joke and not have Crystal figure out what really happened the prior night.

"Well, I should get going," Sayuri said. "I'll see you at the office."

"Thanks again," Alex said.

After Sayuri left Crystal said, "Everything is all set."

"What?" Alex asked, not sure of the context.

"The trip," Crystal said. "We'll be going and spending four nights in Quebec and then driving south to Maine where we will be at the cabin for two more nights and white water rafting on the second day. Six friends are joining us."

"Oh, the trip," Alex said. "That sounds good."

"Are you okay?" Crystal asked.

"Just distracted," Alex said. "I really wish I knew what happened to my truck."

"Check with Bob like you said," Crystal replied. "Hopefully that'll help put your mind at ease and they can get whoever did it."

"I'm hoping it's Sandra," Alex said.

"That would be convenient," Crystal laughed.

Alex noticed Crystal's suitcases in the other room. "Do you have a photo shoot?"

"I did, but it got cancelled," Crystal sighed.

"Cancelled? Why?"

"Cutbacks," Crystal shrugged. "You know, the economy and all."

If she began to lose work too, he wondered if they would make it through this downturn. From the top of the world to barely surviving. That would be an unfortunate twist.

Alex paused in thought, looking at Crystal. She looked ill. "Are you okay?"

"Sorry, I've been queasy the last few days," she explained. "I figure I must have gotten some food poisoning or have some kind of bug." Her eyes widened and she ran to the bathroom and vomited.

Alex went in with her, helping her by holding her hair and letting her know he was there. "Is there something I can do? Do you want to go see the doctor or something?"

"No," Crystal said, still hugging the basin of the toilet bowl. "If this continues for another day or so maybe. But not today."

"Are you sure?"

"I'm sure," Crystal said.

"What did you want to do today?"

"Let's go see about your car," Crystal suggested, and that's exactly what they did. Alex took another shower and got dressed. The two then went to the garage his SUV was towed to and got the good news that the tires and windshield could be replaced that day and that there was no other apparent damage. The windshield was covered by insurance. The tires he had to pay for. By nightfall he had his car back and things were back to normal. At least for the moment.

22

Monday morning Alex went to work and stopped at the security desk to see Bob Healey. Somewhere in the depths of his mind he knew that it was probably some punk kid who vandalized his truck, but he could not accept that. It was Sandra who had done it. He was certain of that.

"Morning Bob."

"Morning Alex. How was your weekend?"

"Not very good," Alex said. "Someone vandalized my car."

"The Mercedes?" Bob said, wincing. "That's horrible."

"Yeah, I came out of work Friday night and the tires were slashed and the window shattered," Alex said.

"You mean it happened here?"

"It did," Alex said.

"Oh, I'm so sorry," Bob replied. "That never should

have happened."

"That's life, right?" Alex shrugged. "Any chance you can pull the recordings from Friday and see who did it?"

Bob waved Alex closer and then whispered. "I wish I could, and don't let this get around, but with all the construction the security cameras outside of the building don't work."

"Seriously?"

"The wires were severed by accident. Some kind of foul up on the schematics. It's all hush hush right now so people will still feel safe. We've got extra trucks driving around for security instead, but obviously not everything is caught."

"When do the cameras go back up?" Alex asked.

"If you ask me, they should have been back up right away, but probably not until construction is done and they are ready to repave."

"Oh well, it was worth a try," Alex said. "Thanks anyway, Bob."

"You'll keep that to yourself, right?"

"My lips are sealed," Alex promised.

Alex went upstairs and into the office. He was welcomed by Sandra's signature—and most insincere—belly laugh. Just hearing her back in the office was enough to turn his stomach and set him in a foul mood.

After she made him cancel his meeting last week, Alex had rescheduled it for this morning. He figured it was his own little act of rebellion—he would postpone it, but it would be so early when she got back that she would hardly even have an opportunity to check her messages and either miss it or not be prepared for it.

He checked his messages, went through his morning routine, and then grabbed the materials and headed to the conference room. His former team all made their way in and they were ready to begin. Alex took attendance and began the meeting, but three minutes into it the door opened and Sandra walked in. She said she was sorry she was late, but she glared angrily at Alex, as if upset that he dared begin the meeting without her.

Alex carried on as if she was not there, figuring she would cut him off or let him continue. He did offer a quick recap. "I was just explaining that we were here to discuss the timing of whether we removed features and the savings to testing, but the added efforts for development, versus keeping the features in and having additional testing time."

"It has already been decided that the features are coming out," Sandra said.

"Why?" Alex asked, not caring if he upset her. "By removing features we are decreasing the appeal of the release to the market. Development also has been designing the game with the features included and would need a major redesign to take them out."

"The decision has been made," Sandra stubbornly replied.

"The decision may have been made, but I don't believe

those making the decision were aware of all of the facts," Alex said, challenging Sandra.

Sayuri shot him a warning glance to try and get him to tone it down slightly.

Doug picked up where Alex left off. "To do a redesign would be a waste of time. We already spent the time building it, and taking features away would double our efforts. The features should stay. Alex is exactly right."

"You and Alex do not dictate the direction of these projects," Sandra said, glaring at Doug now.

"Surely if you brought this to the attention of the people who made the decision, or if the right people were in the room when the decision was being made, this would not even be an issue," Doug said.

Alex tried to hide a grin—most unsuccessfully. His team was coming to bat for him. For all Sandra would do to say that everything was his fault, his error, his inadequacy, they were pointing out that he was right and she was wrong.

"Doug and Alex are right," Everton said. "I can get the code now rather than wait for it. There is more to test, sure, but we can get started now instead of trying to rush it in time for the holidays."

"This is not up for debate," Sandra said. "The decision has been made."

"It was the wrong decision," Sayuri said matter-of-factly. "I will be advising my father that this topic should be reopened and that you are ignoring the advice of the subject matter experts. He will be most interested by that."

Alex's eyes widened in surprise at that. Sayuri rarely went to war like that. She always offered help, but bringing her father into it so publicly was an outright declaration that Sandra had to change the way she was acting or things would get worse for her. Sandra was flustered, growing more angry by the moment.

"That will not be necessary," Sandra said. "So it is the belief of everyone here that features should not be removed to speed up production?"

Everyone nodded or expressed their agreement.

"Fine. Alex, update the documentation accordingly."

"We'll need sign-off this week," Doug said. "We already wasted a week. My team began trying to dumb down the code because of this new direction. We can't waste another week."

Alex was loving this. Doug was making his case for him. They wasted a week because Sandra was out and refused to allow them to meet. This was priceless.

"I'll distribute the document for review and then sign-off," Alex said. Of course he already had it revised and ready to go. This was the outcome he wanted and he was prepared for it.

"Get to it," Sandra said as she stood up and stormed out.

Everton whistled. "Sayuri, remind me never to piss you off."

"I merely felt that Sandra was not willing to listen to the expert opinions of her people," Sayuri said. "I meant no disrespect."

"Don't worry, we all know what you meant," Everton said as he got up and began to walk out. He patted Alex on the back. "That's a win in our column. A few more and maybe things will get back to normal."

"We can hope," Alex said.

"Don't hope, fight," Doug added. "I'm tired of that bitch changing everything just because you wrote it. Screw her."

"Thanks guys," Alex said as they both walked out leaving him and Sayuri alone. "And especially thank you."

"You do not have to thank me," Sayuri said.

"I do need to let you know how much I appreciate it," Alex said.

"Anytime, Alex-san."

Alex walked back to his desk, drafted up the minutes and sent them to Sandra for her mandated review before sending them out. He loved the line that he knew she would take out: "S. Takato advised that she would inform T. Takato of the Development and Testing opinion that removing features would be more time consuming and detrimental than keeping in for release." He also added a follow-up to receive T. Takato approval to keep features in the game as expected. Not surprisingly, Sandra took both out with her revisions.

Alex made the modifications she requested and emailed the minutes out along with the revised document. He included a note indicating:

> *As we discussed in the meeting, development needs the new Interim Solution to be signed off on as soon as possible so that their efforts can continue. Please review and provide any feedback you may have to me by the end of the day.*

Five minutes after sending the email he got an instant message from Sandra asking to see him. He should have expected something like that. How could she resist the urge to lash out at him after being away for a week and then having a morning meeting where he got exactly what he wanted? His fortunes would never last if she had anything to say about it.

He knocked on her door and she kept her back to him, ignoring him.

"You wanted to see me?" he said, just in case the knock was not apparent enough that he was there.

She did not turn around but tersely said, "Sit."

Alex sat down and waited. She was still working at her computer, ignoring him. He looked around, trying to find something to distract himself. She had a mini-white board with some notes on it about things she needed to do. He was surprised not to see "chastise Alexander Adams" on it.

He looked around for something else to take his attention. She did not have any pictures, any decorations, anything personal at all. The closest she had were her keys that had been tossed on her desk and slid to the far end away from her computer.

Sandra rotated her chair around and slid over to him. "Why did you send that document out?"

"I sent it out for people to review," Alex said.

"It's not ready for sign-off yet," Sandra said.

"I didn't send it for sign-off. If you read my message I asked for feedback."

"You sent it prematurely," Sandra said. "I sent a retraction and told everyone to ignore it."

"You did what?" Alex asked.

"The document does not have my edits yet. You will not send it out until it does."

"Why not get feedback so that those and your edits can all be incorporated at once?"

"You will wait until I give you my edits!" Sandra said, her face growing red. "This document is inadequate and poorly constructed."

He so wanted to argue that point. The document was perfect. He would willingly hand this document to Brett Curran or Dan Greteman and suspected that they would both feel it was superbly written.

"When do you think you can get that to me?" Alex

asked.

"When I'm done with it," Sandra snapped.

"Any estimate or idea?" Alex pressed.

"This is my first day back. I'll get to it eventually."

The way the meeting went emboldened Alex. "You heard Doug in there. He needs it right away. His team needs to know how to proceed and not waste time."

"Why did his team make changes last week?"

"Because you made it clear that features were coming out," Alex reasoned.

"But that document was not signed off on," Sandra said. "You should know better. Without a signed off and approved document they should not have done anything."

"If I had the meeting as planned everything would have been fine."

"You will not meet without me being present!" Sandra shouted. "Now leave me alone. I have work to do. I'll get this to you when I feel it's good and ready. Everyone should be on hold until I do."

Alex shook his head in disgust. She always had to get her way. Even when everyone else knew she was wrong. He got up and walked out of her office. Sayuri saw the fury on his face and intercepted him, pulling him with her into an empty conference room and closed the door.

"Are you okay?"

"She's at it again," Alex said.

"You're not going to do anyone any good if you lose your temper again," Sayuri said. "You need a break, a distraction."

"What did you have in mind?"

"Your schedule is not as busy as it used to be. Let's do lunch."

Alex snorted at that. Once he would be double or triple booked almost every hour. Now he was lucky if he had a single meeting a day. Of course he was free.

"Lunch sounds good. Let's do it."

But it wasn't lunch that they had. This time there was no drinking involved. Sayuri drove them back to her place where she said she would make them something and give them a chance to talk without being overheard. They had sex on the couch, had lunch, and then she led him into the bedroom where they had sex a second time. Alex was so angry at Sandra and disgusted with the way things were going that this time he did not even think about Crystal or worry about betraying her. This time it was all about getting past the anger and having the distraction Sayuri suggested.

23

She was positively giddy. She should have known, or at least suspected, but it had taken her completely by surprise. She knew that they had discussed this in the past, but both had agreed to wait, to focus on their careers. Especially with her being a model. But maybe the timing was perfect. If her photo shoots were being cancelled due to the down economy, then maybe some time away would be okay.

She couldn't wait to tell Alex. She wanted to see how excited he would be. She hoped that with everything he was going through at work that he would be excited. This was the kind of news that had a tendency to turn things around. This was a life-altering announcement. His issues with Sandra would hopefully not be as consequential anymore. They had more important things to think about and to worry about. They had a reason to make sure they were well off. If that meant getting paid a solid salary to be the secretary to a witch, then so be it.

She heard his car and lit the candles on the dining room table. The lights were out, with the candles as the only source of illumination. Alex opened the door and called out, "Crystal, hun, are you there?"

"In here," Crystal said.

Alex walked into the dining room, bent over and kissed her. "What's all this?"

"A celebration," Crystal replied.

"Did the photo shoot get rescheduled?"

"No, better than that," she said. "You should sit down."

"Okay," Alex said, sitting in the chair next to her, taking her hands in his and gazing into her eyes. "What is it?"

"It's wonderful," she said, feeling her eyes well up with tears.

"Crystal, tell me," he said.

"We're pregnant."

"We're... we're having a baby?"

"We are!" she cheered as she leaned into him and threw her hands around his neck, kissing him. "Isn't it wonderful?"

"Are you sure? How did you find out?"

"Oh, those are the words every girl wants to hear," she

said as she playfully punched his shoulder.

"Sorry," he said. "This just took me by surprise. I'm happy. That is, if you're happy. You wanted to wait because of your career."

"I'm really happy," she said. "This feels good. I'm excited. The timing is perfect."

"So how did you find out?"

"You know the queasiness?"

"Yeah," he said.

"Well, I finally had enough and decided to go see the doctor today. I figured she'd give me a pill that made me feel better. Instead she broke the news. We're pregnant!"

"What about modeling?"

"My calendar is clearing up as more advertising is being cut. Companies just don't have the budget right now. Everyone is feeling the pinch."

"I hear that," Alex said. "So good timing."

"Very good timing."

"Do we have to cancel our trip?"

"I asked about that. We'll be fine," Crystal said. "I can still go."

"That's good. I'm looking forward to getting away."

"Me too," Crystal said. "Four nights all alone with you in Quebec sounds perfect."

"A little romance, a little adventure," Alex said, looking

forward more to the rafting trip. Though the time in Quebec would be good. Especially with everything that has been going on with Sayuri, and now a baby, spending time alone with his wife was just what he needed.

"Let me get dinner," Crystal said.

"No, you sit. You deserve some rest. I'll get it."

Crystal let her hand flow over him and caressed him as he got up and began walking away. She then brought it to her chest and giggled. She was so happy. Everything was so perfect. Even with the reduced assignments and what that would mean for them they still made great money and had plenty saved up for a rainy day. They would be fine. They would be better than fine. They would be a real family.

24

After Alex walked into the kitchen he shut his blackberry and phone off for the night. This evening was just for him and Crystal and he did not want to be bothered by anyone. Their night was a good one. They ate, drank some wine, and made love by the fireplace—it was a bit warm for a fire, but it was romantic and both loved it.

In the morning when Alex turned his phone back on he saw that he had missed several calls and had three voicemails. All three were from Sayuri who sounded desperate to reach him. He listened to them and grew upset by the time the last one finished—she was on her way back to Japan, recalled by her father.

Sayuri's voice did not seem pleased with the decision. Alex could not help wonder of Sandra had something to do with it. After Sayuri had come right out and threatened Sandra with going to her father, she suddenly was recalled. It seemed far too coincidental for his liking.

Alex tried dialing Sayuri back but he just got her voicemail. He left a quick message. "Sayuri, sorry I missed your calls. Phones were off last night. Call me back when you get this."

He then went to work where he tried to keep his eyes and ears open for any news that might corroborate his theory. When Sandra arrived, she looked smug and pleased with herself. If that wasn't confirmation he did not know what was.

He got an email from Barney asking to see him in his office when he had a chance. Alex wondered if there was more bad news about to be delivered. He walked over to Barney's office and knocked.

"Alex, come in. Close the door behind you."

Alex stepped into the office and closed the door. "What's up?"

"I trust you heard about Sayuri?"

"I did," Alex said.

"It was a shock to us all. Her being summoned back so quickly like that. I wish I knew what happened," he said. "But until we find out whether she's coming back anytime soon or not we have to operate under the assumption that she is going to be gone for awhile."

"Okay," Alex said, keeping it simple.

"Of everyone we have, you would be the most qualified to come in and take over her projects. You think you're up to it?"

"Did you discuss this with Sandra?" Alex asked, knowing that his new boss would likely have quite a few objections to him tripling his project-load.

"She knows I have recommended giving you these projects back, yes," Barney said.

That did not mean she approved, she was just aware. "I have no problem taking the projects back on. But what is my role?"

"What do you mean?" Barney asked.

"Sayuri did not report in to Sandra. She ran the projects as she saw fit. Under Sandra I do not have as much flexibility."

"Well, those projects will be with Sayuri's team, so we'll work something out," Barney said. "Do you know Yuzo and Sumio well?"

"We've been in some meetings together, but Sayuri usually represented her people," Alex admitted.

"Well you should get to know them better. Yuzo is the lead developer and Sumio the lead tester. I'm sure you'll all get along just fine."

"What about my existing projects?" Alex asked. "Will Sandra still be looking to run those instead of me?"

"We'll leave those as is," Barney said. "But take advantage of this opportunity. If you show Sandra that you can run the Japanese projects and succeed with them, maybe she'll sign off on that promotion of yours."

Alex still had no faith of that, but at least he had six new projects without Sandra's oversight. "Thanks Barney, I won't let you down."

"I know you won't," Barney said.

Alex was anxious to get to work and get back to working the way he wanted to. The way Sandra had him running his projects was more like maintenance and upkeep. He could do that in ten minutes. The rest of the day he dove into the projects Sayuri had been managing. Three of them had originally been his, three were ones Sayuri brought with her from Japan.

He did feel bad that he was suddenly taking over something of hers, but he also suspected that she would rather he handle these and do them well than trust someone else—especially Sandra—to take the lead. He was still anxious to find out what happened to her and why she was recalled to Japan.

Alex spent an hour going through Sayuri's files and notes and then scheduled a meeting with the Japanese leads who were in the states. Sayuri had her own Elissa who had been working for her in Mayumi Aihara. Alex wished he still had Elissa instead of Mayumi, but she was quite helpful, promised to get everyone together, and asked him several times if there were additional materials he wished to review. He found her quite thorough and detailed. An asset to Sayuri and her team.

The rest of the Japanese team included Yuzo Kanai, the lead developer, and Taichi Omata, another developer. Sumio Uwabo was the lead tester, and Seiji Yoshida completed the group as the Marketing Director. Unlike Alex's former team where Sabrina Stanley only became involved near the end before a game was launched, Seiji was involved from the very beginning so that he could include promotional ideas and market factors into the actual design of the game—the theory was that he was closest to the market demand and desires of the people and was considered a crucial member of the team.

The meeting went well. Alex found everyone quite receptive, willing to take direction, and ready to work. They offered opinions if asked, but otherwise kept things professional and followed a strict chain of command. After the meeting Mayumi remained behind to ask Alex if he wanted her to write and send out the minutes for him—she wanted to make sure she was clear on his expectations and protocol.

Alex said that that was fine, but he wanted to take a look at them first. Even as he said it, after seeing how badly Sandra ripped his minutes to shreds, and made him feel incompetent all of the time, he knew he would endeavor to make only a change or two, if that and let her have her own style and maintain her pride in her own work. Whatever she produced would probably be fine.

"Mayumi, I do have a question for you," Alex said.

"Of course, Alex-san," Mayumi said.

"Do you know why Sayuri was recalled?"

Mayumi glanced from side to side as if checking to make sure nobody was listening. She then leaned forward and whispered, "I'm not sure it would be appropriate to say."

"Please, Sayuri is an old friend," Alex said.

Mayumi bit her lip, weighing the pros and cons of speaking, but then nodded. "She was recalled for dishonoring her family name."

"Dishonoring her name?" Alex said, wondering how she had done that. Was it because Sayuri had spoken out against Sandra? Or did her father catch wind of the fact that she was having an affair with a married man? "How did she do that?"

"She was disrespectful to a senior executive," Mayumi said.

So it was Sandra. "Thanks Mayumi. That'll be all." Sandra had seen him with allies and then took steps to remove them from the game. Like a chess match, his Queen was just claimed by his opponent. He wondered how long before Doug Malone and Everton Taylor found their heads on the chopping block, too? If Sandra had her way, probably soon.

But he could not worry about that now. He was back, he had his own projects, and if his other people were in danger, perhaps Barney would let him bring them with him. All he needed was his foot in the door again. He'd find a way to swing the door open and end this nightmare once and for all. Nobody else would be a victim of Sandra. He swore it.

25

Things at work were better now that Alex was running Sayuri's team, but Sandra still did her best to put him down as often as possible. While he was happier, there was still an underlying annoyance and feeling as if he could explode like a raging volcano at any moment. When it was time for him to leave for vacation he was anxious and ready to go—just itching to get away from Sandra.

Before he left he had had another run in with Sandra. He had been having a dialogue with Everton on one of his lesser projects. As part of Sandra's directive, for those projects he copied her on the correspondence. She came back indicating that Alex should not have been bothering Everton with questions and concerns such as that—it did not matter that Everton had initiated the discussion—and that Theresa already had the answers to those questions. The only problem: Theresa was on vacation. Alex asked Sandra if she knew, but Sandra said no and that he should wait until Theresa got back.

He hated the new system she had in place. Once there were two project managers assigned to everything. For the things he could not make, Elissa attended in his stead. If he was not there she knew what was going on. If she was not there, he did. Under Sandra's approach, everyone had a project of their own and had no cross-over or correlation so that if the lead was out the project essentially came to a stand still. The approach made no sense to him.

Behind her back he and Everton had a call, finished their discussion, and moved forward. What Sandra did not know would not hurt her. If he had to wait for Theresa, then when she came back he was gone, so essentially the project would be put on hold for two weeks for a simple question.

When he left he had Mayumi take control of the projects he inherited from Sayuri. In the time between him taking over and leaving for the trip he came to respect her work ethic and thoroughness. She would do fine making sure things did not fall apart while he was out. For the projects under Sandra, technically she was to look after them, but Alex asked Elissa to do so under the radar and make sure Sandra did not do something to screw them up.

With business done, he was home, the SUV packed, passports ready, and he and Crystal were driving to Canada on their vacation. This would not be their first time heading to Quebec. They went together when they were in college. Crystal loved it. Alex just wished he could pronounce the names of the food on the menus and understand what he was ordering—French definitely was not a language he was comfortable with.

He knew how excited she was though, and he was determined for them to have a good vacation. There was a lot of walking up and down huge hills to get to various parts of the city with little shops. There were restaurants they tried. There was a horse and carriage ride they took. There was a fort that they took a tour of. There was even a haunted tour of the city where they learned all about hangings and improprieties and had a spooky guide trying to frighten everyone and make them believe in ghosts.

Most of the time though they spent in their room, enjoying the time together and alone. Alex was quite pleased by the fact that the only time they were actually dressed was when they left the room. Other than that they were in bed, in the hot tub, in the shower, on the couch, or even once on the porch at night without a care in the world that someone might see them.

The trip was good and Alex was glad that he and Crystal had the time together away from the stresses of work and alone. He did not usually enjoy the more romantic destinations, desiring instead the thrill and adventure, but he did really enjoy spending time with his wife. They even bought some souvenirs for babies so that the future addition of the family would know that he or she had been here, too—even if being there was in their mother's belly.

After leaving Quebec they drove back to the states and into Maine. They reached the cabin shortly before dusk and found most of Crystal's friends already there—friends may not be the most accurate term. Two of the women were fellow models, both of whom had boyfriends, and another couple who were friends with one of them. All eight of them shared one cabin. Alex and Crystal got the loft to themselves. The beds were not big enough for both to sleep on together, but after being in Quebec all alone they figured a night of sleeping in a bed next to each other was acceptable. There were two rooms downstairs that had already been claimed and another bunk bed in the living room that doubled as a couch—that was where the last couple would sleep.

Since they were rafting in the morning the first night was fairly low-key. People had eaten on the road and went to bed early. Alex saw coolers of supplies for the following day and night though. It looked like everyone was planning a huge barbeque and party after the rafting trip was done.

He did not sleep well on the small bed. His legs were too long and hung over the edge. But it didn't matter. Rafting was in the morning. He could hardly wait, and he was not disappointed as the morning came and they were ready to go.

The trip was not on a big-water day, so it was not as dangerous or exciting as some of the trips he had been on. The biggest rapid was only a class 3, but he did not mind. This was a good little river. They got off to an early start with the rapids and then spent the later part of the day just drifting and relaxing. The tour guide brought out "duckies" at the mid-way point—blow up kayaks—for people to paddle around on. Alex and Crystal took a duckie and paddled off on their own for a while. While they did, their boat was tipped over—the guide got in the water and had the main raft go vertical. One of the models lunged, pulled at the line, and forced the entire boat to tip over. Alex did not mind getting wet, but was glad he was on the duckie at the time.

It was a good day. A peaceful end to the trip. He had a lot of fun. But beneath the surface something was still lying in wait, bubbling just out of reach, just waiting to come out. He did not even know how close the anger was to boiling over, but as the night turned into morning there had been no controlling it—everyone was able to witness just how on edge Alex really was.

26

Crystal's friends had brought coolers full of food and drinks for the night. When they got back to the cabin everyone was in the heat of the moment—laughing, joking, retelling stories of things they had done during the day, and overall enjoying themselves. There were stone circles for fires that were quickly fired up and the food began being heated—steaks, shrimp, chicken, and skewers of assorted meats and vegetables.

As day began shifting to night and the cool air crept in, people moved chairs closer to the fire for warmth and atmosphere as they laughed and joked by the fire while cooking their dinners. The process was slow-moving, but nobody cared. They were all having fun.

Another cooler was brought out with beer and the group began drinking—heavily. Alex had never had a taste for beer and refrained—he preferred either something stronger or a non-alcoholic beverage. As a group broke off and began a drinking game, he and Crystal and one of her other friends just stayed by the fire and watched them. None of them needed to join in—they were fine on their own. Besides, Alex was sure a drinking game would be bad news for the baby—at least at this stage of the pregnancy.

Before long the group was growing loud, laughing at everything, and began acting foolish and doing stupid things. The friend of Crystal's told them that when they checked in they were warned not to "get rowdy and destroy the place." Alex assumed that drinking and doing crazy things was par for the course at the cabin. He wondered what the poor people who ran this place had to put up with each day after checkout. Whatever it was, he would make sure that his and Crystal's areas were clean to show some respect.

As the night went on Alex was beginning to feel out of place. He was not the only one. Crystal and her other friend did as well.

"Do you get the feeling that we're not really included in the group?" Crystal asked.

"They couldn't care less that we're here," the friend added.

"Good thing it was my trip," Crystal sighed.

"You had fun, right?" Alex said.

"I did," Crystal said.

"That's the important thing."

"Yeah, well, it would have been nice if we all could have done something together."

"I agree," the friend replied. "They're acting like a bunch of drunken fools."

"I think I'll call it a night," Crystal said.

"Are you sure?" Alex asked.

"There's nothing over there that makes me want to stay up," Crystal said.

Alex watched the people and their drinking game for another minute or so. He wondered what Crystal's friend would do if they both abandoned her. Would she go to bed too or go join the game? It didn't matter. Not his concern. He followed Crystal into the cabin and up to the loft.

They both got into their respective beds and Alex lay there—uncomfortable—staring at the slanted roof for a long time as the sounds of laughter, shouting, and swearing from outside filled the room. Finally he decided he would just read. He had brought several books with him for the trip in case he had the chance to read—all suspense or mystery novels. He took out a little mini-reading lamp, turned it on, and opened the book.

He glanced over at Crystal. "Will the light bother you?"

"No, I'm fine," she said.

That was enough for him. He began reading. This particular book was about a group of people on a camping trip, but one of them was not quite what they seemed and people began getting murdered. As he read it was the classical blend of suspense and doubt as the survivors tried at first to figure out what happened to their friends, but then began to realize that they were in danger, and then tried to figure out who exactly they could trust—was it one of their own or was it someone else in the forest with them? Alex had his own idea, he always did, and was pleased to see that he was right. He always seemed to know just who the killer was in books like these. But he still enjoyed them.

While reading he paused, wondering what would happen if it were him in the book and making the decisions. Would he be able to get away with it? Memories of a child with lifeless eyes looking up at him from the bottom of a cliff flashed before his eyes. There were always mistakes made. Or the killer seemed to want to be caught. They acted suspicious, as if they wanted people to know what they had done. To take credit for it. The image of the car soaring off the road flashed before his eyes.

He did not want credit. He also did not feel guilty. Perhaps that was a fundamental flaw. If he stopped to admit it, three people were dead because of him. Three people. Shouldn't he feel remorse? Shouldn't he feel something? But he did not. The boy deserved it. The drivers annoyed him. He knew his actions were excessive and at some point a rational and normal person would have stopped and not done what he had done, but if he really stopped to admit it, he did not regret either action.

But the beauty was he did not get caught. He did not

have the need for people to know what he had done. He did not have the guilty conscience where he could not live with what he had done. The closest he had come to guilt was when he had cheated on Crystal with Sayuri, but even then he did it again. It obviously did not bother him too much, and like with the other two incidents, he had gotten away with it.

Was that the allure? The thrill of doing something and not being caught? He did not think so. Not being caught was just a requirement. He liked his life. He liked his marriage. He had big plans for his future. If he was caught running someone off the road, or cheating on his wife, then his future plans would be in jeopardy. He could not allow that.

But his future plans were in jeopardy. He did not want to think about her, but he would he driving home tomorrow and back to work Monday. Sandra was screwing with his future, too. She was using her own bias, her own hatred, and trying desperately to sabotage his life. The image of the lifeless boy came to him again. Could he make his problem go away? After all, what the boy and the driver who cut him off paled to what Sandra had done to him. Didn't she deserve to suffer for all of the pain she inflicted on him?

As soon as he had the thought he put the book down and turned the light off, thinking about Sandra. With the boy he was alone and had the opportunity. There was no thought, just reaction. To the car that cut him off it was blind fury, but again opportunity. Even with sleeping with

Sayuri the first time, they had been working late and alone and if someone did not damage his car they never would have done what they had. It was opportunity.

Was there an opportunity with Sandra? At work they had others around. Anything he did at work would undoubtedly get him caught. He had no desire to get caught. He wanted to remove a thorn in his side, not ruin his life. So how then?

His thoughts were distracted as the door was pushed open below with such force that it slammed into the wall, followed by loud giggling. He sat up and looked over the edge of the loft down at a couple of people who were practically tearing each other's clothes off as they stumbled into the cabin. They landed on the bunk beds and the laughter was replaced by moaning, groans of pleasure, and screams of orgasm.

Alex glanced at Crystal and saw that she was awake and looking at him. He reached out to her and she took his hand. They held hands while listening to people having sex below. There would not be sleep this night. It would be a late night. Then his eyes widened, and he had an idea.

It was so simple. Complex, truthfully, but so simple. If he did not have an opportunity, he would need to make one. That was risky, and he would need to make sure he did not leave evidence behind that could point the finger at him—after all, with his obvious disdain for Sandra, obviously he would be a suspect even with an air-tight alibi. But the trick was to have her removed from the picture without anyone knowing she was really gone.

He was grinning as the images of what he would do swirled through his mind. He did not even hear the door open a second time and people laughing as they came across the two people having sex, or the screams of the people as they realized someone else had seen them. No, he was enthralled with images of seeing Sandra suffering, in pain, and dying. Of course, thinking about it and doing it were two completely different things. He would entertain the idea, but unless he was pushed too far, he doubted he would do anything about it. Just an innocent exercise in wishing someone you hated was dead. At least that was the way he looked at it.

With images of her dismembered and bloody corpse in his mind, he actually fell asleep, still holding Crystal's hand. Surprisingly, it was undisturbed and peaceful sleep. The loud and drunken cabin-mates completely forgotten about.

In the morning Alex was wide awake and ready to go. Crystal was dragging a bit—she had not been able to sleep well at all with all of the noise from the prior night. There was not much for breakfast, just eggs and bacon, but it was enough to scramble large amounts for the group to get them some food before hitting the road for the day.

Alex had some eggs and bacon and then got to packing. With the vacation essentially done he was anxious to get on the road and get home. Going on vacation he never seemed to be in a rush. He enjoyed the drive and stopping at places along the way. But on the final day he just wanted to push, to get home, to unpack, to get things back to normal as much as he could.

He was fortunate to get the first shower of the morning—that had been easy since most of the people in the cabin were hungover or still passed out. Crystal had gone in after him. He had his things packed with the exception of his book and waited for her to tell him she was done with her suitcase as well.

Alex sat and read while he waited. He had gone outside, sat by the lake, and felt relaxed as he enjoyed a good book away from everyone and everything. But that did not last.

"Morning."

Alex turned and saw one of the guys from the group. He did not know the man's name, but recognized him as the guy who kicked the door in and had sex on the bunk bed below the loft the prior night. "Morning," Alex replied.

He walked closer to the water, holding a loaf of bread, and looking out at the geese. He opened the bag and began tossing some chunks of bread to the birds. They all rushed for the bread, like a giant competition to get the food, and pecked at it to try and snag the bread before one of the others did.

234 • CLIFFORD B. BOWYER

He began backing up slowly, heading to a picnic bench and sat down on it, tossing bread on the ground. The geese left the water, came to land, and began waddling after the bread he was throwing.

A few other people began coming outside, milling around the bench and watching the guy feeding the geese. Crystal came out, too. She made her way to Alex and sat down on the arm of his chair.

"I'm ready whenever you are," she said.

"Did you have to say goodbye to anyone?" he asked.

"We're good," Crystal replied.

"I'll go load the car," he said. As he stood up he saw the guy who was feeding the geese getting up on the table, looking like he was about to pounce, dropping bread right below him. "What the hell is he doing?"

A goose made its way up, standing right below him now, claiming the bread. The guy slowly put the bag of food down and began waggling his fingers in anticipation as he prepared to spring.

"Don't even think about it," Alex said.

The guy glanced back, questioningly.

"You hurt it, I hurt you," Alex emphasized.

"Alex, don't," Crystal cautioned. "He's not going to hurt it."

"He better not," Alex said.

With a devious grin that spoke volumes, the guy turned away and dropped on top of the goose. The goose honked and then tried to flee as the guy began chasing it, his arms held out. He got close, but as his hands brushed the feathers of the bird Alex was putting his old football training to good use, tackling the guy and forcing him away from the bird.

"What the hell are you doing?" the guy shouted.

There were other screams Alex could hear. Some people were laughing. Some were shouting to leave each other alone. Some to stop clowning around. He tuned them out.

"I told you not to think about it," Alex said as he slammed the guy on the ground.

"Let me up!"

"How do you like it?" Alex said, his hands now clutching the guy's head with his knuckles digging into pressure point behind the ears.

"Let me the fuck up!"

Alex lifted the guy's head off the ground and slammed it down as hard as he could. He felt hands on him then, pulling him off.

"Leave him alone."

Alex felt feral, wanting to tear them apart for daring to stop him from defending the goose. He hated people who preyed on the innocent and defenseless. This guy was the scum of the earth. He deserved a little suffering for what he had done. Alex tried to pull himself free, but stopped when he heard his wife.

"Alex, stop!"

Alex froze and the two guys let him go. Alex turned and saw Crystal, looking horrified.

"He was just having fun," she said.

"People shouldn't hurt animals," Alex said. "You should treat them with the same respect you want people to treat you."

"Whatever, man," the guy said, rubbing the back of his head.

Alex felt like jumping on top of him again and pounding on him. People like this would never change. He could see him going out of his way to hit an animal on the side of the road. People like this deserved what they got.

"Alex!"

"Fine," Alex said as he turned and walked back to the cabin. "I'll get our stuff so we can get out of here."

As he walked away he could hear Crystal apologizing for him. Apologizing to that monster. It turned his stomach. He couldn't believe she was taking the side of someone so cruel, so heartless. He was glad this trip was over. It was time to get back to reality. He had enough with this so-called relaxing.

27

The trip home was a quiet one. Alex did not want to talk about what happened and Crystal seemed to be trying to avoid it. Alex wondered if she was scared of him and what he had done. He hoped she knew he would never hurt her, but he was just not able to stop from trying to protect the goose. The innocent needed to be protected. Just like he would always protect Crystal and their unborn child.

When they got home they both went about unpacking and getting things back to normal. At least they began talking again, discussing things that they needed to do, and even a few references to how much fun they had in Quebec and rafting—Alex knew the morning was purposefully being overlooked and he was perfectly content with that.

Deciding to check to see if there was anything pressing from work—for the projects he was able to run his way, not the ones for Sandra—he logged into his work account remotely and scrolled through the letters. Unless something jumped out at him he intended to read it and respond Monday morning. But it was always good to be prepared for what to expect.

He had a letter from Elissa's home email account. He thought that was odd and opened it up. As he read, he felt his spirits sag and began growing angry again. He picked up the phone and dialed her number.

"Hello?"

"Elissa, it's Alex," he said.

"Oh, hey, how was the trip?"

"Never mind that. I just got your email. What happened?"

"Sandra stopped by my desk and asked what I was working on. When I mentioned that I was looking into one of your projects she flipped. She practically dragged me away from my desk to a conference room, told me that I was not to help you under any circumstances, and when I said I was just making sure there were no issues that needed to be resolved, she told me that she could not have people going behind her back and that my services were no longer required."

"She fired you. Just like that?"

"Just like that," Elissa said.

Crystal walked in, looking curious. "Who got fired?"

"Sandra fired Elissa because she was checking on my projects."

Crystal's eyes sagged. She shook her head. "Nothing that woman does surprises me anymore."

Alex went back to the phone. "What are you doing now? Do you have money saved up?"

"A little," Elissa said. "I lost a lot when the market crashed."

"I can't believe she did this," Alex said, pounding his fist on the table. "You have kids to take care of. Responsibilities."

"I'm trying to get unemployment while I look," Elissa said.

"You need to file a grievance, or suit against Sandra and the company," Alex suggested. "There were definitely no grounds for termination. This is crazy."

"That's Sandra," Elissa said. "I see now what you were going through."

"You mean you missed the memo of how much crap I was taking?"

"No, not that," Elissa said. "But I wasn't talking back, arguing, or fighting to keep things the way that they were. Sandra seemed to actually like me and was not treating me like she did you at all. I found this so unexpected."

"It's because you were helping me," Alex said. "I bet if you were helping anyone else—Theresa for instance—she wouldn't have even said a word."

"I'm not disagreeing with you," Elissa said.

"I'm so sorry that you became a casualty of her and my little feud."

"It was bound to happen sooner or later," Elissa said. "I'd be willing to bet that all of us will find ourselves out of a job before too long. Junador was first. Sayuri next. Now me. I think Doug and Everton are on her hit list, too."

"It can't get to that point," Alex said. "I won't let it."

"You are the last person who can stop it," Elissa said. "But I do appreciate how you've always looked out for me. Keep me in mind when you find a new job and need a right hand man you can trust."

"Or woman," Alex corrected.

"Or woman," Elissa agreed.

"Good luck with whatever you're doing. Keep me posted. Let me know if there is anything I can do to help."

"Of course," Elissa said. "For now, I think I'm going to spend some quality time with the kids and take advantage of the unemployment. I'll probably get bored of that in a few weeks, but for now the kids deserve to have me around more."

"You all deserve it," Alex said. "It's important to put the needs of the kids first. Good luck."

"Thanks, to you too. I have a feeling you're really going to need it."

Alex hung up and Crystal walked over and hugged him. "I can't believe she did that? It's more than just me. She's destroying lives."

"She's a wicked, evil, heartless woman," Crystal said. "People like that get what's coming to them in the end. Karma."

Alex did not want to wait until she got what was coming to her. He was going to give her exactly what she deserved. The thoughts of doing something to her on the trip was mere fantasy. But she had gone too far this time. She always went too far. There was no turning back now. She had to pay for her actions. He would see to it that she paid dearly.

28

Alex was at work bright and early Monday morning. He was one of the first in the office and while he was alone he actually walked into Sandra's office, sat down at her desk, and studied her belongings. He looked at her mug that she used to refill her coffee every morning and how it looked like she did not even rinse it out after each use. He looked at her jar of sugar sitting next to her printer. He looked at her board and the notes she had on there. He looked at the disorganized and scattered piles of documents that filled her space. He looked at how dirty the few barren spots of the desk itself was—as if the filth of the woman was smeared into the wooden surface. He looked for anything that would be redeeming in some way, anything at all that let him know she was actually human and had a heart, but he did not see anything that would lead him to that conclusion.

He got up from her desk and returned to his, glad for the orderliness. His desk was clean, organized, and pristine. Even without being here for a week he did not see any dust or anything out of place. How people could work effectively when they were so disorganized blew his mind. How *she* could be expected to lead him when she so clearly was inferior in every way made it even worse.

Alex logged into his computer, accessing his email and went through his normal post-vacation routine of going through the messages. Like always he began with meetings to make sure his calendar was updated and he knew how to judge his time properly. He saw a meeting request for 8:00 PM on Wednesday with Tokyo. He glanced at the invite and from this office only he and Sandra were on the call. He wondered why there would be a meeting without any of the other key resources, but did not think about it too much. Instead he focused on the time and the opportunity that that presented. Wednesday night. Here. Alone. With Sandra. He would be ready.

Knowing that this would all come to an end Wednesday night actually made him a little giddy. By the time other people began arriving, he was smiling and in a great mood. They all attributed it to his vacation and how this was that period of time where the daily grind did not get to you because of all the good will built up from the vacation. People could think whatever they wanted. He knew why he was so happy—so excited.

Mayumi stopped at his desk after she arrived and bowed slightly in greeting. "Welcome back Alex-san."

"Good morning, Mayumi," he said pleasantly.

"I trust your time off was beneficial?"

"Most beneficial," Alex said. "How were things here?"

He was expressing pleasantries, but Mayumi took it as a request for a debrief. She actually had one prepared and handed him a synopsis of where their projects were and any developments that occurred within the past week. She spoke about each, giving a quick overview and emphasizing anything that he should be aware of. She was most thorough. A tremendous asset. He was quite fortunate to have her.

"Thank you, Mayumi. Clearly I left the team in great hands."

"I am pleased I was able to adequately cover for you," she said with another bow. He actually thought he caught her blushing, too. "I do have another message for you, from Sayuri."

"Yes?"

"She is back in the states to clean out her apartment," Mayumi said. "She told me she would love to see you if it was at all possible to fit it into your schedule before she returned to Japan."

Alex turned back to the computer and opened his calendar program. "Looks like today is pretty open. Is there anything I'm missing?"

"No meetings, no," Mayumi said.

"I'll take an extended lunch then. If a meeting request comes in, try to schedule it either before or after that."

"Of course," Mayumi said. "Welcome back."

"Thanks," Alex said. He was glad Sayuri was here. He felt horrible about how she was so quickly recalled to Japan and they had not had a chance to talk in person. Today he would rectify that. If only she could come back and they could work together again like they did. Of course, that means surrendering her team and only working for Sandra again, but that would not be an issue after Wednesday.

"So you're back."

Alex froze at the voice. There was something about it, like someone dragging their fingernails across a chalkboard. How he hated that voice and everything about the woman. He forced a smile on his face and rotated his chair around to look up at Sandra.

"Of course I'm back," he said. Then he decided to try and throw her off a bit while still being polite yet sarcastic. "Did you miss me?"

"Hardly," she said. "I actually had a week of peace and quiet around here without your insolent tongue trying to challenge me at every turn."

"At least we're finally being honest with each other. You don't like me. I despise you. But we have a job to do."

"Not for long, if I have my way," Sandra said with a smirk at the thought. "It's just a matter of time and you'll be gone, just like I got rid of Elissa, Sayuri, and Junador."

He couldn't believe she was admitting it. "We both know it's me you want. Why not come after me first? Why go after them?"

"Because you care about them, and seeing them suffer makes you suffer," Sandra said as she laughed in delight. "Besides, they all took your side. They acted against me to help you. To think, that little bitch thought I wouldn't notice her working on your projects while you were away."

Alex's eyes narrowed. How petty she was. If only he had some way to record this conversation. He was sure Human Resources would be most interested in it. "I always knew you were a monster, but you really are heartless, aren't you? Elissa has kids to support."

"That's her own mistake for having them," Sandra shrugged.

He knew she was an old, single, bitter woman who never had a family. He also recalled the stories of how she did not tolerate the "bring your child to work" events or people taking time off because their kids needed them. She had no understanding or respect for parents at all. He was willing to bet that she would even give him a hard time when Crystal was in labor. She'd refuse to let him go. Well, she wouldn't be around to stop him from being a good father.

"It's a shame, really. You're the kind of person only your own child could love. Obviously you'd rather devour dreams and souls than take joy in seeing others happy. To think, when you're gone there won't be anybody who will miss you."

"When I'm through with you, there won't be anybody to miss you, either," she said. "Anyone, but me, who will dance over your grave."

Alex picked up his pen and began rotating it through his fingers. He did not want to let her bother him, he was too happy to let her get to him again, but she was outright telling him how she was purposefully trying to stress him out so much that everyone in his life would turn on him as he grew more and more irrational and upset. He saw the way Crystal looked at him after the incident with the goose. If he went any further, was pushed any further, would she leave him? Would his team ultimately leave him?

"I'm not done yet, either. I've only gotten started. Everyone from your team is going to be cut lose," Sandra gloated. "I've already planted the seeds. They will be gone, replaced by contracted labor without benefits. Its just good business in this economy. Seeing you squirm and feel guilty about it is just an added perk."

"You would really do that? Go after everyone, even people who just worked with me?"

"Anyone loyal to you will learn the folly of their ways."

He had heard enough. Wednesday was not soon enough. Something had to be done, and it had to be done now. He stopped twirling his pen and flicked the cap off.

"And there is nothing that you can do about it? The last

248 • CLIFFORD B. BOWYER

thing you'll see before you leave is how everyone whose life's you touched were all destroyed. All because of you."

"Guess we'll start with you then," Alex said though Sandra, who was in the midst of one of her deep belly laughs did not hear his comment. Alex stood up, raising the pen in an uppercut motion and striking her in the fleshy part of her head under her chin. The pen broke through skin, up into her mouth. Sandra's belly-laugh ended at once as she began screaming in agony, blood spurting.

Alex pushed her to the ground and stood over her, her eyes glaring up at him with a combination of pain, shock, and terror. He raised his foot and brought it down on her head, stomping as hard as he could. Others in the office had heard the screams and were coming to look to see what happened. Alex was committed now. So much for getting away with it. As long as he went this far he might as well protect the people he loved by making sure she was dead and buried and unable to hurt anyone ever again. He raised his foot again and again and again, slamming it down and watching as blood spurted, bone cracked, and Sandra's life faded from her eyes.

Those around screamed, or ran for help, or backed off from him. None approached to help. Why would they? Who would ever want to help a witch like Sandra Murphy? She did not engender loyalty or respect. She managed with a microscope and tried to lead with fear. Nobody would care that she was dead.

He sat back down in his chair, swiveled around and went back to his email. There was a lot to read when one got back from vacation. There was no turning back now. He saw the opportunity and took it. She was dead, and though he knew he would pay for it, he was genuinely happy by what had happened. She had just kept pushing and pushing and pushing and he was not going to take it anymore. He was glad he had done it. It was over. Finally over.

"What, are you ignoring me now?"

Alex was confused. That certainly sounded like Sandra. He glanced down at his hands, expecting to see her blood all over him, but his hands were clean. He looked to the left and saw his pen sitting on his desk. Had it all been a dream?

He swiveled around, half expecting to see her lying dead on the ground, a pool of blood flowing out from beneath her and gushing out of her crushed face, but instead she was standing over him, glaring down at him.

"Just because you took time off doesn't mean the rest of us can stand around waiting for you when we need something."

"What do you need?" Alex asked, confused because the vision, or whatever it was, had been so vivid. He had even tasted the metallic taste of her blood as it initially sprayed into his face and mouth when he had rammed the pen through her chin. Yet here she was, obviously alive and unharmed.

"With Elissa gone I need to redistribute her projects. Barney feels that you would be the ideal choice to take them on. I need to know whether or not you can handle it. *I* don't think you can."

"I would be happy to take the projects on," Alex said. "Express my gratitude to Barney."

Sandra looked disappointed. She wanted him not to be able to do it. But then she perked up. Alex felt like he could read her mind at that moment. She saw him failing with added responsibility, and she could use that as her soap box to show that everything she said about his incompetence was true. He would not give her the satisfaction.

"Well, fine then," she said. "I expect the transition to be seamless and you to pick up right where Elissa left off."

Alex wanted to say something about how if she wanted that she should not have fired Elissa, but he saw where arguing got him. He knew the pen was nearby. He was not about to throw his life away. If anything, the vision showed him what to avoid.

"I'll take a look and let you know if I have any concerns."

That threw her for a loop. She actually looked taken aback. He was going to consult her? Alex loved it.

"See that you do," she said as she turned and walked away.

He could play nice until Wednesday. Wednesday was not that far away.

29

As Alex was leaving for lunch to go meet Sayuri at her apartment, he stopped to talk to Bob at security. Bob was waving to him as he was heading by.

"Hi Bob, how are things?"

"Can't complain," Bob replied. "How was the trip?"

"It was good," Alex said. "Had a little incident at the end with someone who was being cruel to animals, but it takes all kinds, right?"

"You can say that again," Bob replied. "A lot of crazy people in the world. Speaking of which, make sure you lock you car and take your keys with you."

Alex looked quizzically at Bob. What an odd comment. "I always do," he said.

"That' a relief," Bob said. "There's been a few cars reported as stolen. With the *you-know-what* out, I feel pretty helpless."

"Any idea what's happening?" Alex asked.

"You ask me, it's the construction workers," Bob said. "They're in the lot all day working. They see a car with keys and decide to go for a joy ride."

"Could be kids," Alex added.

"Could be," Bob nodded. "But mark my words, we'll get the *you-know-what* working again and catch those construction guys at it."

"Good luck with that," Alex said. "Heading out for awhile. I'll catch up with you more later."

"Sounds good. Have a good day."

Alex walked out the door and made his way through the parking lot. He saw Sandra drive by. He had never seen her car before. It was a tan Cadillac. He grinned politely but she actually turned her head away and looked in the opposite direction. He wished she had not seen him. Now she would know he was taking a long lunch and give him grief over it. But what else was new?

He got into his truck and began driving to Sayuri's. He saw the oil light on, and realized that with the trip to Canada and back he had gone more than the recommended amount. He took his phone out, clicked the button for contacts, and scrolled through the list looking for the dealership. The phone rang three times before someone answered.

"Mercedes service."

"Hi, this is Alexander Adams, I was wondering if I could schedule an appointment for service."

"I have an opening tomorrow morning."

"Mornings don't work for me," Alex said. "Could I drop it off in the afternoon, maybe get a rental car, and then pick it up the following morning?"

"We can do that. Which day works for you?"

"Let's see," Alex said, pausing to think about his schedule. "Wednesday would be perfect."

"What do you need done?"

"Oil change, tire rotation, and just a basic diagnostic to make sure everything is okay."

"Can you get it here by 3:00?"

"I could drop it off during my lunch break," Alex said. "How about one-ish?"

"Perfect," the man said. "See you Wednesday."

Alex hung up. He should probably have Crystal bring her car in too. He did not know when the last time she had her car checked out had been. But Wednesday was good enough for him for the moment. Instead of a rental car he always could ask Crystal to pick him up or arrange to have someone meet him with the Rubicon, but this way he was not inconveniencing anyone.

He pulled into the apartment complex and Sayuri and walked to the intercom, pushing the button for her.

"Hello?" she said through the intercom.

"Sayuri, it's Alex."

"Alex, come on up," she said, sounding excited. The buzzer rang and he opened the door.

Alex jogged up the stairs and out to her floor. She had the door open and was standing in the doorway waiting for him.

"This is a surprise!"

"Mayumi said you were back and wanted to see me," Alex said. "I also didn't like the way you were called back to Japan so suddenly."

"That's my family for you," she said.

"Was it my fault?" he asked as she closed the door behind them.

"What a silly thing to say. No," Sayuri said. "Sandra lodged a complaint that I was disobedient and uncooperative. My father refused to listen when I got home. He was just upset. Koichi listened though and he got our father to agree to hear what I had to say. He's actually proud of me."

"So why are you packing up?"

"Until things calm down I will work from the Tokyo office," Sayuri said. "It is for the best."

"At least you have that option," Alex said.

"Is it really bad?"

"She fired Elissa while I was on vacation because she was checking on my projects," Alex said.

"If anyone has dishonor, it is her," Sayuri said. "I trust you are on your own with my projects?"

"I am, yes," Alex said.

"Mayumi tells me that you are running them quite competently."

"I do my best," Alex said.

"I am glad. People will see what you are capable of and not just listen to the lies she is spreading."

"So when do you go back to Japan?" Alex asked, looking at the boxes.

"My flight leaves at the end of the week," Sayuri said. "I find I am not very motivated to pack and leave."

"Were you packing just now?"

"No, I'm ashamed to admit I was sleeping," Sayuri said. "The flying back and forth has been impacting my sleeping habits."

Alex laughed. "You look as if you are ready for a photo shoot with Crystal. I would never know you just crawled out of bed."

"Thank you, you humble me, Alex-san," she said. She picked up a bottle of prescription pills. "Actually, these have been wondrous."

"What are they?"

"Sleeping pills," she said. "I got them before I left Japan. Just one and I am ready to pass out in no time at all."

"That good?"

"That good," she confirmed.

"Mind if I try a couple?"

"Are you having trouble sleeping?"

"Ever since Sandra became my boss I find that I have

trouble with most things," Alex said.

"Definitely then, help yourself," Sayuri said.

Alex opened the lid and poured a few pills into his hand. He then shoved them in his pocket. "Thanks. I'll see if these help."

"There are other things that can help you relax," she said.

He could read the longing in her eyes. He did not feel right doing anything. It was not right for her. She deserved better. "How about I treat you to lunch?"

"I will let you treat me to lunch if you let me offer you a massage first."

"A massage?" Alex asked.

"You look like you could use one," Sayuri said. She then added, "I am quite good."

"I bet you are," he said.

"I will get ready with some warm towels. You go into the bedroom, take off your clothes, and lie down."

"Do I really have to take off my clothes?" Alex asked, not sure if he would be able to resist if he was naked with her.

Sayuri giggled. "It is necessary for a proper massage."

"Well, who am I to argue with propriety?" Alex said as he walked into the bedroom. He looked at the bed and knew that the last time he was here with her they had made love in that bed—also during a lunch break.

He sighed and then loosened his tie, took it off, and

then unbuttoned his shirt. Everything he took off he folded and set down on a chair she had in the corner. After taking off the rest of his clothes he went and lay down on his stomach on the bed.

Sayuri walked in, dimmed the lights, and lit several candles. She then turned on her stereo and he heard the sounds of water trickling. "Is that nice and soothing?"

"I like it," Alex said.

Sayuri got onto the bed and onto his back. Alex could feel her bare skin touching his and did not have to look to know that she had taken her clothes off, too. She put one wet and warm towel on his lower back and another one that she placed over his eyes.

"Just relax," she whispered into his ears. She then began slowly massaging his shoulders, working her way down his back, moving around to massage his arms, his legs. She was right, he felt so relaxed and she was quite gifted at this. Then he felt her lips brush against his neck. Before he realized what he was doing he was moving into the kiss, their lips joining. By the sound of trickling water, he turned over, she mounting him, and rhythmically moving with the sound of the water until both were sweating, drained, and satisfied.

30

As the day began to wind down Alex called his wife to let her know that he was taking her out to dinner that night and that he wanted to do a little shooting too. He wasn't sure if she would want to go with him to the club, but he'd let her make the choice.

When he reached her she had actually just begun thinking about dinner, so it was perfect timing. She said she was not in the mood to shoot but he could go after they ate. He told her to pick whatever restaurant she wanted and they would go. She picked a Thai restaurant that was new and she wanted to check out.

Alex was glad that at dinner Crystal seemed to be over the incident with the goose. The way she looked the other morning was something he hoped never to see on her face again.

At dinner he shared information from work, including how Sandra stopped by his desk and gave him back some of his projects now that Elissa was gone. He mentioned his suspicions that she was hoping he would fail, and Crystal thought that it was likely, but they both agreed that having the projects back was better than not having them. Things might actually be looking up.

He also told her that Sayuri was back for the week and that maybe they should all get together before she went back to Japan. Crystal thought it was a wonderful idea and said she would call Sayuri and set something up. Alex let her know that any night but Wednesday would be good because he had a call with Tokyo and would be working really late. Crystal promised to take care of it.

After he dropped her off he took a couple of guns and ammunition and drove down to the club. Just like every other night he went there he was the only shooter. Alex unlocked the closet to grab some more targets and noted that all of the tools and things he saw were still there. He wondered if someone worked on the grounds and what exactly they did.

Curious, he took a flashlight from his glove compartment and took a walk along the grounds of the club. He usually only spent time in the main building and rarely visited the rest that the club had to offer. There was a pond for fishing, a range for archery, a section for skeet shooting, as well as a little target course for matches.

Alex walked to the rifle range and up onto the large mounds of dirt that were behind the pits to stop the bullets from going beyond. He would never risk walking on these during the day, but at night there would never be any shooters on the rifle range. He looked over the back of the pits and saw mounds of dirt, wild growth that looked like it had not been mowed or tended to in decades, and further back what looked like a swamp.

His curiosity satiated, he went back to the main building, still empty and alone, and shot for about and hour before locking up and calling it a night. As he drove home, the details he had imagined on the trip for dealing with Sandra were all coming together. He knew what he had to do. He knew just what he was going to do. It all seemed too easy. It couldn't possibly be that easy, but everything was just coming together. He knew arrogance and cockiness would not serve him well right now, but his plan was coming together nicely, and by this time Wednesday night Sandra Murphy would no longer be a thorn in his side. He could not think of anything that made him happier than that. At least not at that moment.

31

When his alarm went off Wednesday morning Alex was already awake and just pushed the button to turn it off. It was not that he was anxious, in fact he felt calmer than he had in a long time, but he also did not feel as if he could sleep. It was the little details that kept flowing through his mind, the intricacies that he needed to have go right so that what he was planning would work.

He was not worried, but began thinking about what would happen if things began to go wrong? He began creating contingency plans for his plans so that regardless of what happened today he would be ready for the worst.

Alex took his shower and got ready for work as usual. He went downstairs for breakfast with his wife, who already had the juice poured for them.

"Morning, hun," he said.

"You didn't seem to sleep too much last night," she said.

"Lot on my mind," he said.

"About tonight?"

He knew she meant the meeting with Tokyo, not what else he was doing, but he just nodded and said, "Yeah, a lot going on tonight."

"I'm sure you'll do great," she said, coming over and kissing him on the forehead.

"Thanks," he said. He got up and walked over to the tin where they kept their prescription medicines—the tin was a souvenir from one of their first trips together, and anything that required daily use they put in there. He opened it up and pulled out a container and unscrewed the lid, looking down at the white granular substance.

"Are you having trouble again?" she asked.

"Not as bad," Alex said. "But might be worth taking with me just in case."

"Better to be safe than sorry," she said.

He had to agree. He had intense stomach cramps that had only gotten worse for three days. He kept thinking that he would be fine in the morning, but every day he felt even more tender to the touch and with intense throbbing in his stomach. Crystal demanded that they go to the doctor and he said that it was because Alex was blocked and unable to go to the bathroom for some reason. The prescription was like a super-laxative. In an hour after taking it he was able to have his first bowel movement. An hour after that he was running to the bathroom every few minutes with diarrhea so intense he thought he was going to die. But the following morning he had no pain.

"Oh, hey, I made an appointment to drop the car off today."

"Do you need me to pick you up tonight?" Crystal asked.

"No, they said that they could just give me a rental car," Alex said. "I hope it's not a piece of junk. What would the neighbors think?"

"Ooh, the scandal," Crystal teasingly replied, acting horrified. "I think they'll get over it."

Alex glanced at his watch. "I should get going."

"Have a good day."

"You too," Alex said. "It should be a really late night tonight. Especially with Sandra with me. I'll wake you up when I get home?"

"Okay," she said. "Good luck."

"I need it," he said with a grin. He kissed her and then headed out to his car. He had to get to work earlier than everyone else. The first part of his plan depended upon it. He needed to create his opportunities.

Alex reached the office in record time. Traffic was not even bad. During the night he half expected being stuck in traffic, behind an accident or something. But he was here and early. With a few pleasantries to Bob he headed up and scanned the office floor, grinning to see that he was alone.

He walked over to Sandra's desk, lifted the top of her sugar jar and poured the equivalent of several big heaping spoonfuls of the prescription laxative in. He looked in and silently cheered triumphantly when he saw that the sugar and medicine was almost completely indistinguishable. Of course her coffee would not taste as sweet, but that would just make her use more.

Closing the lid and pocketing his prescription Alex left Sandra's desk as he had come across it and went to his desk where he began his normal routine. Within the hour people began arriving and the day went through the normal routine. He did not focus on Sandra, but actually had an almost sixth-sense today, knowing every time she got up, how distressed she looked, and saw her running quickly. The laxative was definitely working.

Alex picked up a report that he had finished yesterday and walked over to her desk—knowing full well she was in the bathroom at the moment—and knocked on the door. Even with her not there it was not an unusual act. He always knocked on doors of empty offices as he walked in—just in case someone saw him go in they could never accuse him of barging in. He did, after all, announce himself.

Alex stepped into the office, frowned in case anyone was watching as if he expected Sandra to be there. He then searched her desk to find a post it note and wrote, "Here is the report you wanted to review, Alex," and posted it on the cover page. He put the post it note pad back where it was, set the report down on her vacant chair so she would actually see it, and palmed her keys—which were at the end of the desk where she always tossed them—and slid them into his pocket as he was turning around to walk away.

He returned to his desk and to work. About ten minutes later Sandra came up behind him. He knew she was there. He could hear her panting.

"This is only one report. Where is the synopsis of everything Elissa was working on?"

"Oh, I'm sorry, I'll have that later today. I thought you'd want that one as soon as possible though."

"Fine," Sandra said as her eyes widened and she bolted.

Alex grinned. He remembered all too well what that particular prescription did to people. Before he left for lunch he told Mayumi that he was dropping his car off for service and might be a little late. Since he had a night call he didn't expect anyone to mind, but just in case someone was looking for him he wanted her to know. She thanked him and said she would cover for him.

As he was leaving he stopped by the desk to see Bob. "Any luck catching the car thieves?"

"Not yet, but I still have my suspicions," Bob said.

"You going to pull a fast one and catch someone in the act?" Alex asked.

"Not until *you-know-what* is working again," he sighed. "But we're keeping a close watch on the lot."

"Good," Alex said. "Hopefully you'll catch them. See you soon."

He walked out and decided to take a walk along the outer walkway. It was different from how he usually got to his truck, but it was also the direction where he had seen Sandra driving from that day at lunch. He hoped that she usually parked in the same general vicinity like he did. He grinned when he saw her car on the end spot by the exit.

Alex walked past it, *accidentally* dropping the keys on the ground by the driver's side door. He never slowed down, never looked back. If anyone saw him walking they would not think twice about what he was doing. But he hoped that keys dropped right by the door would be too much of an allure for whoever was stealing cars.

This was one part of his plan that required a contingency plan. He needed her car to be gone. If the car was gone, and she was gone, nobody would think anything about her getting in trouble here. The entire office would practically be in the clear. In fact, people might even think she took off and just vanished. A missing person, not someone murdered. One of life's little unsolved mysteries. But someone had to be drawn to the car and try to take it.

Alex got into his truck and drove away. As he went out the exit he glanced at her car and saw the keys right there. If someone saw it it sure would be tempting. Of course, someone might be a good Samaritan, pick the keys up and turn them in to Bob at the front desk. Whatever happened he knew he was hoping for the best but prepared for the worst.

He brought his car in and saw that they had a blue van with absolutely no options ready for him as his rental car. He frowned, said he was shocked that a Mercedes dealer would give such an inferior vehicle to its customers, but deep down he was thrilled with what he had. The van would be perfect. He half expected to have to shove Sandra into a trunk. This would be much more practical.

Before returning to work he went to the hardware store and bought himself some industrial gloves, boots, and a new outfit that was perfect for working. He also got a lantern-flashlight, plenty of batteries, and some rope. He put all of those in the back of the van and then returned to work after stopping at the drive through for some fast food to eat.

When he pulled into the parking lot he saw that Sandra's car was gone. She either had to go someplace and found her own keys by the door, or the car thieves worked quickly. As Alex was walking to his desk he saw Sandra rushing to the bathroom again and grinned—definitely the car thieves.

Back at work, people began clearing out around 5:00. By 6:00 he and Sandra were the only two people left on the floor. A little after 7:00 he heard her walking away from her desk. He did not want to assume she would be gone long. She did not look like she was still running to the bathroom.

But he took the opportunity to do the next part of his plan.

He walked over to her desk, knocked like he always did, dropped the synopsis on her chair and flipped the lid of her mug open. There was still coffee in there and he was glad to see that it was steaming—she was keeping a warm cup to nurse throughout the day in preparations of having to stay awake for the meeting at night. He was never a lover of coffee and was surprised how much she could drink. But her consistent patterns helped him do what needed to be done.

He reached into his pocket and pulled out a small container he had. He took the top off and poured the contents in—the crushed up remains of Sayuri's pills. He put her lid back on, slipped his container into his pocket, and turned around. Sandra was standing there.

"What are you doing?" she demanded.

Alex reached down to her chair and picked the report up. "Here's the summary you asked for."

Sandra pushed past him, snatching the report from his hand, and sat down. "You should have waited until I was here."

"I'm sorry, I thought you would want it right away. Usually I leave things on people's chairs if they are not here." As he was speaking he wondered if she had seen him. Was she suspicious? Was he not quick enough?

"That's inconsiderate and unprofessional. Do not do it anymore."

"Okay," Alex said. His fears were set aside as she reached for her mug and took a sip. She hadn't seen anything.

"Was there something else?" Sandra demanded.

"Nope, nothing," Alex said.

"Then get back to work. We're not paying you to stand around and do nothing."

Alex could counter that he was on salary and was not paid for staying five hours late anyway, but he turned and returned to his desk. Her opinions did not matter. It was only a matter of time now before she did not matter at all. Everything to this point had gone perfectly. It seemed almost too easy. He knew he still had a long way to go before he would be done, but as he thought about how each and every thing he planned had been pulled off flawlessly, he wondered why people who did this always seemed to get caught? It had to be the emotion, the guilt, the need to confess. He would have none of that.

The meeting began and ended with little issue. Alex did most of the talking for their end. Sandra was struggling to stay awake and kept chugging her coffee like she needed an intravenous line of it to keep herself awake. Little did she know that the more she drank the more tired she would become.

When the meeting was over she had been sleeping and snoring slightly. Since it was a video conference, Tomiro and Koichi Takato were both upset by the lack of respect that Sandra was displaying. Alex could tell just by how they shifted their attention to her with angry glares that they were upset. He could probably walk away and do nothing and she still would have found her final days at Creative Visions Entertainment—it never paid to fall asleep on a call with the CEO for Takato Games and his senior executives and show that you did not care enough to even stay awake for their meeting. It was a tremendous lack of respect. At least, Alex thought, when she was gone the Japanese executives would not consider her missed.

Alex looked at her, seeing her sound asleep, and then walked over to her desk. He reached into her purse and took her cell phone out and placed it in one of her desk drawers. He then walked back into the conference room and sat down where he had been during the meeting.

"Sandra?" Alex said, leaning over and touching her shoulder.

She snapped up. "Don't touch me!"

"I'm sorry, the meeting is over," he said. "You look exhausted. You should go home and get some sleep."

Sandra looked at the LCD television that was now off and winced. "I missed the meeting?"

"I made apologies for you. Said you were having a really long day and were not feeling well."

"Yes, that's true," she said.

Sandra stood up and almost toppled over.

"Are you okay?" Alex asked.

"I don't know what's wrong with me," Sandra said. "I feel so drained. So exhausted."

"Maybe the pressure of the job is getting to you," Alex said.

That woke Sandra up. She glared at him. "You would like that, wouldn't you?" She then stormed out of the conference room. Alex followed behind and saw that her bravado only lasted a few steps before she slowed down and was shuffling her feet to her desk.

Alex followed behind. "You really look tired. Maybe you should call a cab or someone to give you a ride?"

"I am perfectly capable of driving myself," she barked.

"Okay, well, I'm heading out. See you tomorrow," Alex said.

She snorted and went to her desk. As he gathered his things and logged out of his computer he saw her pick up her purse and jacket and head to the elevator. She was moving slowly, but she was leaving. Alex waited until she was on the elevator and then went down the stairs.

He got to the ground floor and saw her walking out the building. Security was already gone. This time of night the doors would lock behind him as he stepped out. He just had to make sure he closed the door and it was secure. He did so and walked out into the parking lot. Sandra was standing, looking around, unable to find her car.

"Is everything okay?" Alex asked.

"I don't remember where I parked," she said.

Alex looked at the lot and did not see a single car. "Are you in the garage like me?"

"I'm never in the garage," she snapped.

"Sorry, just trying to help," Alex said as he began walking away to go to his car. He paused, turned, and looked at her. "You know, Bob told me that there have been some stolen cars reported lately. Do you have your keys?"

"Of course I have my keys," she said as she reached her hand in her purse. She felt around and then looked horrified. "I must have left them on my desk. They aren't here."

"Are you sure?" Alex asked. "If your car is gone, maybe you dropped your keys."

"You think?" she asked.

"You should call the police," he said.

"Don't tell me what to do," she said, but she reached her hand in her purse again for her phone. She did not find that, either.

"Are you going to be okay?" Alex asked as he backed several steps away closer to the garage. "You don't need me to wait for you or anything, do you?"

"My phone isn't here," she said. "Give me yours."

"I'm sorry, my battery died," Alex said. "I usually would charge it in the car, but I have a rental while service is being done. I can give you a lift if you need it?"

Sandra did not seem pleased with that, but she nodded.

"This way," Alex prompted. He watched as she walked toward him, slowly as her feet shuffled around the ground.

He had probably overdone it with Sayuri's pills, but it wouldn't matter in the end.

Alex opened the passenger side door and held it for her, waiting until she got in and then closed the door. He walked around to the driver's side and got in. "Where to?"

"Cambridge," she said.

"That's quite a hike," he said. "I wish my phone was working so I could call Crystal and let her know I was running late. Oh well. Let's get started." He started the van and drove out of the lot, onto route nine. Before he even came close to the Mass Pike she was already sound asleep and snoring. He did not speak again, instead pulling off onto a back road and leaving any route that would possibly go to Cambridge.

Once he was on the back roads he did not pass anyone else. He made sure he drove the speed limit the entire way without fail so as not to draw any potential unwanted attention his way. Within the hour he pulled up to the locked gate of the gun club. Alex looked at his sleeping passenger to make sure she was not awake and got out of the van to unlock the gate. He got back in, drove through the gate, and then got out again to lock back up.

He drove to the main building first where he unlocked the main door and then the closet door to take the shovel out. He locked both up before leaving just in case anyone else came to the club before he left. He opened the trunk, put the shovel in, closed it, and then got back into the van and drove out to the traps of the rifle range.

Alex parked the van as close to the traps as he could and got into the back of the van where he changed out of his clothes and got into the outfit he bought at the hardware store earlier in the day. He also checked the flashlight and walked out onto the dirt mounds and brought the light down to a hole in the ground. It was not the most elegant hole in the world, but he had come the night before and begun digging. He covered it up with a board in case anyone actually came back here—though he doubted anyone had. The hole wasn't as deep as he would have liked it, but he had hit large rocks and had trouble getting them out. Regardless, it would have to serve for his purposes.

With the shovel and light set up he went back to the van and opened the passenger door. He tied Sandra's hands and legs with the rope he bought and then pulled her out of the rental vehicle. The drugs were so potent that she did not even stir as he moved her. He kicked the door closed behind him and walked up the dirt mounds and down the back to where everything was waiting for him.

Alex walked to the hole and set her down in it, face down. He thought about smashing her skull in, about putting a bullet in her head, about stabbing her through the heart. But he did not. Blood would be messy and had a better chance of him being discovered. She was bound and about to be buried alive. He did not need gore to satisfy some sick craving. She would be out of his life and not come back.

He began shoveling dirt on top of her, leaving her head for last. Since there was a body in the ground he did not want a mound to mark her final resting point; he kept packing the dirt and making sure it was flat and completely filled in. Once he had everything but her head covered he shoveled dirt on her face, too. Seeing her being buried felt almost therapeutic. It was almost as if he was burying all of his issues and problems.

After the dirt completely covered her he began adding the rocks. Just because he could not go deeper because of the rocks did not mean he did not get quite a few out. He put them on top of her, leaving the largest one for her head, which he dropped and just let slam into the dirt. He could visualize it crushing the dirt down and braking her skull. The thought made him smile in delight.

With the layer of rocks on top of the dirt he already put in he began shoveling more dirt into the hole, slamming the head of the shovel down to smooth the dirt out and pack it over the rocks. It was easier now, just filling the hole back up. He was done in no time at all and then carefully put the thicket of grass he had cut out back on top. With a little work of the surrounding area it did not even look like the area had ever been disturbed.

Alex used the flashlight to examine the area and check his handiwork. He saw no flaws at all. It was done. Even though the hole was not as deep as he wanted, if she woke up and tried clawing her way out she would not be able to do so. He was confident about that.

He returned to the van and put the shovel and flashlight in it. Rather than starting he decided to make sure he was still alone. He walked over to the main building and froze— another car was parked there. Alex crouched in the bushes, waiting. Who was it? He had never seen anybody when he came here at night, but there was a car. Did they know he was here? Had they seen the illumination of his flashlight over at the rifle range? Were they curious as to what was going on?

He had so many questions but knew that panicking now would only get him into trouble. This was probably just someone coming to shoot. He had already done the hard part. He had gotten Sandra out of the office, buried her alive, and now all that was left was keeping his cool and making sure he got away with it. He knew there was a chance someone might be here. That's why he walked out instead of drove out.

He was there for about twenty minutes, fighting with his own thoughts and internal fears before two men walked out of the club, holding cases of firearms, laughing. They got in the car and drove off without ever even glancing in his direction. Alex waited another five minutes to make sure they had time to get out and not come back because they forgot something. When he was certain that they were gone and not coming back he returned to the van and turned it on. He paused when the lights hit the dirt and he saw his footprints—evidence!

Alex left the lights on and got the shovel back out. He

went to the top of the mound of dirt and glanced over, glad to see that the final resting place of Sandra Murphy remained undisturbed. He knew he would never be able to look again. Going back and checking was one certain way of getting caught. He wished he had done something like strangle her or crack open her skull so that he would not worry about her somehow escaping, but he knew she would not get out.

Using the shovel he backed down from the top and rubbed the head over his footprints and got rid of them. He was glad he noticed. It was a detail that he had overlooked. He certainly did not want anyone at the club overscrutinizing why there were footprints on the dirt behind the rifle range.

Satisfied that he covered his tracks he got in the van and drove back down the dirt path and to the main building. He gathered his work clothes and the shovel and walked to the building, unlocking the door and heading inside. He went to the closet first and put the shovel back where it belonged, and then went to the bathroom where he took his work clothes off, cleaned up, and then got dressed again.

He studied himself in the mirror and was satisfied that there was not any sign of dirt or anything that would give him away. He took the work clothes, put them in the bag he had bought them in, and brought them with him. Before leaving he shut off all the lights and locked the door behind him.

He left the club, locking the gate and driving off without

seeing anyone else. He had done it. He had actually done it.

On the drive home he stopped at a clothes-drop for charity and put all of the work clothes in. The only thing that was left was the flashlight. He considered keeping it since it would be useful to have, but he had paid cash so there would be no trail. He dropped it in a dumpster that was across from the clothes bin and then left it all behind. It was better not to risk having anything be there.

Alex pulled into his driveway, turned off the van, and walked into his house. He went upstairs and saw that Crystal was sleeping. Before joining her in bed he took a shower, leaving his clothes in the bathroom. As soon as he was done and walked into the bedroom, crawled into bed, and kissed her bare shoulder until she stirred.

"Welcome home," she groggily said. "How did it go?"

"Better than I ever could have hoped," Alex said. "Sandra fell asleep during the meeting. I don't think our Japanese partners were very pleased with that. I got the impression that she just buried her career."

"That's good," Crystal said. She turned over, kissed him, then added, "Okay, night, night."

"Night," Alex said, leaning back on his pillow and staring at the ceiling for a minute. It was over. He had done it. It was time to wake up from his living nightmare and see life as beautiful as it had always been. He drifted off, happy, dreaming only pleasant thoughts.

32

In the morning Alex dropped the rental car off and picked his SUV up. He was glad to be rid of it—it was the final piece of evidence. Her hair was in the car. But nobody would ever be the wiser and by the time anyone even thought to come looking for what happened the van probably would have been rented out at least a dozen more times.

Because he picked up his car he got to work a little late that morning. Bob was all too quick to point that out.

"Morning Mr. Adams," he said as he raised his arm, glanced at his watch, and raised his eyebrow at Alex.

"Morning Bob," Alex said. "Late night last night and had an errand to run this morning."

"That's okay, I was just teasing."

"I know, Bob. Have a good day."

280 • Clifford B. Bowyer

"You too," he said as Alex made his way to the stairs.

Alex got up to the office floor and saw people working, talking, or eating at their desks. He had so rarely come in this late it was odd to see all of the bustling activity. He said hello to people as he passed them by and then sat down at his desk to turn on his computer and check his email.

Mayumi leaned on his desk and whispered, "Barney wants to see you."

"Now?"

"He wanted you as soon as you got in," she said.

"Okay, thanks Mayumi." Email would have to wait. He got up and walked to Barney's office, knocking on the door and walking in. "You wanted to see me?"

"Alex, come in," he said. "Close the door."

Alex closed the door behind him and had a seat. "What's up?"

"I got a most disturbing call from Brett Curran this morning. Did something happen last night that you want to tell me about?"

"Nothing that I can think of," Alex shrugged. "The call with Tokyo went quite well. I answered all of their questions and they seemed quite pleased."

"Well, they were, with you," Barney said. "What about Sandra?"

"Oh, that," Alex said, feigning ignorance.

"You don't have to be diplomatic or try to protect her," Barney said. "Brett told me that Tomiro was furious. He said she showed great disrespect and demanded that she be replaced Just what the hell happened?"

"Um, well, she kind of... well, she fell asleep."

"She fell asleep?" Barney asked. He leaned back in his chair, shaking his head. "What a mess this has made. I have to protect her, or take responsibility, but from the call I got, I think both Brett and Tomiro are expecting heads to roll."

"Heads? Plural?"

"Well, one head," Barney corrected. "They were all very impressed with you."

"I appreciate you telling me that. Especially after everything that has happened this year. I trust you know I have always worked to the best of my ability to see this division, this company, and this merger succeed."

"Yes, yes, that has never been in question," Barney said.

"I'm glad to hear that," Alex said. "I'll also say that I do not envy you for this little mess."

"Yeah, thanks," Barney said.

"Is there anything else?"

"No, you can go," Barney said. "Keep up the good work."

"I always do," Alex said as he got up, opened the door and walked out of the office.

That day he ran his projects the way he always had. For the projects he inherited from Sayuri he did things his way without any thought. For the others he also did his way, but copied Sandra on all correspondence—it wouldn't do at all for him to start changing his behavior before Barney made some changes and official announcements about the future of their division.

Sandra did not come to work that day. She did not call in, either. Other than his morning discussion with Barney, Alex noted that not even one person asked about where she was or whether she was joining a meeting. It was like whether she was there or not she was invisible to people.

That night Alex met Sayuri after work and they drove together back to his house where Crystal was preparing a special dinner for the three of them. The three ate, they drank wine, they laughed, and Sayuri filled them all in on a call she had with her father who said that she could stay because it was clear that Sandra was the disrespectful and dishonorable one, not her. The dinner soon became a celebration over her remaining and the speculation of what that meant for the future of the team.

Over the next week, Sandra still did not come to work or call to let anyone know she was staying out. Barney was growing more and more upset by the day. He had been trying to call her, demanding an explanation, but only kept getting her voicemail. In another meeting with Alex he speculated that Sandra was too ashamed by what she had done and must have resigned. Alex did not say anything to either corroborate or oppose Barney's theory, though he thought it weird that Barney would think that without some form of written resignation—she was, after all, still getting paid.

On the Monday of the second week since Sandra stopped coming to work, Barney called Alex into his office again. Sayuri was already back at work by then and wished him luck as he went into the office.

"Alex, there is something I think we need to discuss," Barney said.

"What can I do for you?" Alex asked.

"You once asked me for Karen's job," Barney said. "I was not prepared to offer it then, but I am now. That is, if you are still interested."

"Even after everything that happened with Sandra?" Alex asked. "It's been a rough few months."

"If I have learned anything over these past couple of weeks it is that you were right and she most definitely was not the person I thought she was," Barney said. "To leave the way she did is an outrage. I can't believe how unprofessional she has been. And the way you have picked things right up and got everything organized and back on track? Remarkable. I'm only sorry I didn't see it sooner."

Alex listened and nodded. "There are some things I would need if I were to accept this position."

"Name it," Barney said.

"I run my team my way," Alex said. "I need to know that you have faith that I can run this division and the project managers without questioning my every decision."

"As long as you're producing, you'll have no problem with me," Barney said.

"Elissa and Junador are also coming back. Both with promotions. Elissa can have my old job and Junador can have hers."

Barney winced. "I'm not sure they would want to come back."

"I'll call them, and if they saw no I'll retract this demand. Otherwise, my acceptance is contingent upon your willingness to bring them back."

"Done. Is that it?"

"Not so fast," Alex said. "Sandra nixed my promotion. I should have had an extra week's vacation and raise this entire year. I want that included in the offer of the new position."

"You would be getting a raise," Barney said.

"Yes, but a percentage increase. I want the percentage increase of what my salary would have been. Plus retroactive pay."

"In this economy?" Barney asked.

"Do you want me to call Daniel Greteman and see if he'll sign off on it?"

"No need to call the CFO," Barney sighed. "I agree."

Alex nodded. The fact Barney did agree meant that he was getting pressure from Brett and Tomiro to right the ship. He would do exactly that. "Well, guess we have an understanding then."

"Congratulations," Barney said.

"Thanks," Alex replied. "I appreciate this."

Over the next few weeks things began happening quickly. Elissa and Junador did return. Alex set up a new chain of command with Elissa, Sayuri, and Theresa reporting directly into him with everyone else in the department reporting into them. Sayuri was even generous enough to share Mayumi since Elissa was now running projects and no longer working as his assistant. Mayumi completed her work admirably even with the double workload.

Sandra was never heard from again, but when the video camera surveillance was restored and one of the construction workers was caught stealing a car, the police recovered evidence of nine stolen vehicles, including Sandra's. They attempted to reach her without success. None of her neighbors had any idea where she was or when she was coming home. What happened to her remained a mystery and left it open to rumors and speculation. Alex enjoyed listening to what people thought, but never partook in the gossip.

With Sandra gone and the new job in place Alex felt happier than he had in a long time. He was back to feeling like himself. He was no longer agitated, on edge, or stressed. He ran his team flawlessly and once again was mentioned as an example that the entire company should take note of and emulate in their own departments. Tomiro Takato even flew in from Japan and awarded him with a hand-crafted sword in honor of his success and impeccable business acumen.

The affair with Sayuri came to an end. Without Sandra to cause problems both maintained a close and personal friendship and working relationship, but the lunches and late nights spent in her bed ceased. When Crystal gave birth to their first child, a baby girl who they named Anne Marie Adams to stay with the traditional double A names of the Adams family, Sayuri was named the godmother.

Alex could not have been happier. Work was back to being something he loved. His life was restored to the perfect little world he had always thought it was. And his home life was enhanced with what he thought was the most gorgeous baby girl in the entire world—and coming from the combination of his genes and those of Crystal, a supermodel, who would argue with him?

Life was perfect. Even as he realized that, the memory of what he had done to Sandra drifted into the back of his mind like some kind of crazy nightmare. Sometimes he could not even believe that it had really happened, that he could have plotted, planned, and done what he had done. But he knew that lying beneath the surface of even the most perfect of people was sometimes something darker that they always kept hidden. The trick was never letting people know your inner soul and darkest desires. As he laughed, joked, teased, and charismatically led his life, he knew that he excelled at hiding who he really was from the world.

EPILOGUE

"Okay people, great work on these. Next week I want to take a look at some of the potential games in the pipeline, okay?"

"You got it," Elissa said.

Mayumi looked at her watch and winced. "Alex-san, don't you think you should be leaving?"

Alex looked at his watch then. It was 4:45 and Daycare was closing in fifteen minutes. "Yeah, thanks."

"You're going to be late again," Sayuri said.

"Daycare doesn't like it when you're late," Elissa added.

"I'm sure they'll make an exception," Alex said. "They know Crystal is in the Bahamas on a photo shoot and that I have to work. I mean seriously, who can honestly pick up their kids by 5:00?"

"You better," Elissa said. "They'll get nasty."

"Don't worry, I negotiate multi-million dollar releases daily. How hard can someone who watches children all day be?"

"They're going to eat him alive," Elissa said.

"Absolutely," Sayuri added.

"Let's show some faith for your esteemed leader," Alex said as he got up and walked out. He went back to his office—the same one Sandra used to sit at though he had the cleaners come up and completely scrub it before he moved in and made it his own. It was difficult taking her desk. There were so many bad memories there. But pictures of his family helped brighten it up a bit, and photo shots of places he had been—like white water rafting, mountain climbing, hang gliding, and things like that—covered the rest of the walls so it was as anti-Sandra as possible.

Mayumi followed him to his desk and tapped her watch. "I'll log you off. You go."

"Yes mother," Alex said with a laugh.

"Go!" she ordered.

"Okay, okay, I'm going," Alex said. He grabbed his jacket and rushed down the stairs.

Bob winced and looked at his watch. "Aren't you cutting it a little close?"

"You too?" Alex said, rolling his eyes. "Have a good night, Bob."

"You too, Mr. Adams," Bob replied as Alex made his way out the door and to his truck. He got in, started it up, and pulled out of the lot. In the back seat was a car seat for Anne. Seeing it was like a permanent fixture in the back of his truck. It seemed like it had always been there and the thought of his little angel sitting in it warmed his heart.

He drove to Daycare and glanced at the clock. It was 5:05. Only five minutes late. He walked up to the building and a woman with red hair sat there with her arms crossed and tapping one impatiently.

"Mr. Adams? You're late."

"Sorry, my wife is out of town on business and I had an important meeting," Alex said.

"Oh, and you think your meeting was more important than my life?" she asked.

"Excuse me?"

"That's the problem with parents like you. No respect for others. No respect for common courtesy."

Alex had heard enough. He just wanted to pick up his daughter and go home. "Is my daughter here?"

"Why else would I still be open after hours?"

"It's five minutes," Alex said, growing annoyed.

"Do you tolerate people being five minutes late for your important meetings?" she asked. "I doubt it."

"It's only five minutes," he said again. "I'm doing the

best I can."

"Well your best is nowhere near good enough," she sneered. "See that it doesn't happen again."

Alex glared at her. She looked like she wasn't even out of her teens yet here she was taking this tone with him? Who the hell was she to be so insulting and demeaning?

"Come in, you have to sign something."

"What do I have to sign?"

"There is a fine for being late. This document shows how late you are so you will be billed accordingly."

"For five minutes? Seriously?" Alex asked.

"We take time very seriously," she said, slamming a clipboard down on the desk in front of him. "Sign it."

Alex glanced at the form. "Seventy five dollars? For being five minutes late? Are you kidding me?"

"Do I look like I'm kidding?"

What she looked like was somebody who needed to be taught a lesson. Alex signed the form, pushing the thought away. "Now where is my daughter?"

"In here," she said, walking into another room and picking Anne up out of a rocker.

"You left her unattended?"

"You're the one who is late," the girl said. "You're the bad father."

Alex took his daughter in his arms and whispered to

her, "Daddy has you. You're safe now. Daddy has you."

"Small comfort, a father who is never there when his kid needs him."

Alex glared at the girl. He wondered how many parents this girl traumatized in her job. How many people who were struggling to make ends meet had to pay these ludicrous fines because this girl thought she had some power over people? He held his daughter in his arms and wondered if this girl's influence, her venomous personality, was rubbing off on the children and corrupting them at such an early age. A small grin creased his lips. It was for the children, after all. He had to protect the children.

Also available from Silver Leaf Books:

Fantasy Novels

Jared Angel, Endless War of the Gods
Betraying the God of Light, 1609750772, $19.95
and more to come!

Clifford B. Bowyer, The Imperium Saga
Fall of the Imperium Trilogy
The Impending Storm, 0974435449, $27.95
The Changing Tides, 0974435457, $27.95
The Siege of Zoldex, 0974435465, $29.95

The Adventures of Kyria
The Child of Prophecy, 0974435406, $5.99
The Awakening, 0974435414, $5.99
The Mage's Council, 0974435422, $5.99
The Shard of Time, 0974435430, $5.99
Trapped in Time, 0974435473, $5.99
Quest for the Shard, 0974435481, $5.99
The Spread of Darkness, 0978778219, $5.99
The Apprentice of Zoldex, 0978778227, $5.99
The Darkness Within, 0978778243, $5.99
The Rescue of Nezbith, 0978778251, $7.99
The Responsibility of Arifos, 1609750217, $7.99
Full Circle, 1609750233, $7.99
and more to come!

The Warlord Trilogy
Falestia, 1609750411, $29.95
Falestian Heir, 1609750438, $29.95
Falestian Legend, 1609750454, $29.95

Ilfanti and the Orb of Prophecy, 0978778278, $19.95
Tales of the Council of Elders, 1609750276, $19.95

T.J. Perkins, Shadow Legacy

Art of the Ninja - Earth, 160975039X, $19.95
Power of the Ninja - Fire, 1609750551, $15.95
Heart of the Ninja - Water, 1609750691, $17.95
Truth of the Ninja - Air, 1609750713, $19.95
and more to come!

B. Pine, The Draca Wards Saga

Familiar Origins, 1609750314, $21.95
Plights, 1609750497, $19.95
Coming of Age, 1609750519, $19.95
Glimpses of Destiny, 1609750535, $19.95
and more to come!

Brittany Westerberg, The Destined Trilogy

Into Fire, 1609750330, $19.95
and more to come!

Drama, Suspense & Thriller Novels

Brian Bandell

Mute, 1609750667, $21.95

Clifford B. Bowyer

Continuing the Passion, 097877826X, $18.95
Beyond Belief, 1609750357, $24.95
Snapped, 1609750756, $19.95

Mike Lynch & Brandon Barr

American Midnight, 1609750195, $19.95

Linda McCue

Dark Destiny, 1609750764, $23.95

Justin R. Smith, Constance Fairchild Adventures

The Mills of God, 097443549X, $24.95
The Well of Souls, 0978778294, $19.95

Christopher Stookey
Terminal Care, 1609750292, $19.95

Science Fiction Novels

Clifford B. Bowyer, Gen-Ops
Gen-Ops, 1609750373, $24.95
and more to come!

Stuart Clark, Project U.L.F.
Project U.L.F., 0978778200, $27.95
Project U.L.F.: Reacquisition, 0978778286, $19.95
Project U.L.F.: Outbreak, 1609750470, $21.95

Rob Gullette, Apollo Evolutions
Waking Apollo, 1609750675, $24.95
and more to come!

Mike Lynch & Brandon Barr, Sky Chronicles
When the Sky Fell, 0978778235, $18.95
and more to come!

To order any Silver Leaf Books title, check your local bookstore,
order through our website at www.SilverLeafBooks.com,
or mail a check or money order to:

Silver Leaf Books
P.O. Box 6460, Holliston, MA 01746

Please include $3.95 shipping and handling for the first book and $1.95 each
additional book. Massachusetts residents please add 6.25% sales tax. Connecti-
cut residents please add 6.35% sales tax. Payment must accompany all orders.

ABOUT THE AUTHOR

AUTHOR PHOTOGRAPH BY SUSAN MARIE PHOTOGRAPHY

Clifford B. Bowyer is the creator and author of The Imperium Saga universe. His novels include the *Fall of the Imperium Trilogy*, the young adult spin-off series *The Adventures of Kyria, Ilfanti and the Orb of Prophecy,* the prequel *The Warlord Trilogy, Continuing the Passion, Beyond Belief, Snapped,* and *Gen-Ops.* Bowyer graduated from Bryant College with a degree in both Management and Marketing, and received his MBA from Babson College. Bowyer continues working on developing future installments of The Imperium Saga and Gen-Ops novels. He resides in Massachusetts, where he coaches and plays softball.

www.CliffordBBowyer.com